THE TRAINING OF A DREAM WARRIOR

DOUG DRAKE

WestBow Press books may be ordered through booksellers or by contacting:

WestBow Press
A Division of Thomas Nelson
1663 Liberty Drive
Bloomington, IN 47403
www.westbowpress.com
1-(866) 928-1240

ISBN: 978-1-4497-6101-1 (sc)
ISBN: 978-1-4497-6100-4 (hc)
ISBN: 978-1-4497-6102-8 (e)

Library of Congress Control Number: 2012913520

Printed in the United States of America

WestBow Press rev. date: 08/02/2012

Leo, a shy ten-year-old boy living with his divorced mom and his brother, Blaine, and some friends, stumble onto a nighttime gathering of dangerous teenagers in an empty field where they normally play. This and another unexpected meeting that results in the death of two kids lead Leo and his friend, Amanda, on a search to understand why his strange dreams about extraordinary creatures and mysterious symbols are coming true. Leo is on a spiritual journey he knows very little about, but he is eager to find answers with the help of his friends.

CHAPTER ZERO

Why Dreams

Do young boys have scary dreams? Leo did. He was a quiet, small for his age, but athletic, ten year old boy with light brown hair. He didn't have trouble sleeping, he slept well, but his dreams had begun to trouble him.

Often after waking from his troubled slumber, he would wonder if there was meaning, or purpose in his perplexing dreams. His anxiety about his dreams grew when they didn't stay in the world of soft pillows and warm blankets. The people, places, symbols, and giants he saw in his dreams began to enter his waking world. It was the dream of the kidnapping of his brother Blaine that scared him the most. Were his dreams a premonition, or a foretelling of things to come?

A mighty King named Nebuchadnezzar was once troubled by his dreams too, and was willing to kill in order to find the meaning behind his strange midnight musings. The seer, Daniel, correctly foretold that his dreams were from El Elyon, and the interpretation of the dreams would come from the Most High. The seer was given the correct meaning of the dreams, but understanding would not come till the end.

Thousands of years have passed.

Another seer must be trained, to bring understanding, and to awaken those who sleep.

CHAPTER ONE

The First Rescue

Leo stared at the building from across the rain-soaked street.

It looked to be abandoned, with no sign of life or light coming from anywhere inside. The two-story, broken-down, castoff utility building looked hopeless and tattered against the star-filled sky. Leo got nervous just staring at it from across the street. He wondered if anyone was watching him as he considered whether he should try to force his way in. He knew he had no choice, but he was afraid of who or what he might find inside.

He couldn't be sure why, but he felt certain that his brother, Blaine, had been lured inside. He needed to find a way to get in. He needed to get his brother out before it was too late.

What is this building? What is going on in there? Who would take Blaine? Why? Is Blaine in danger? Is there danger for me?

Leo struggled with these thoughts as his eyes ran back and forth from the broken windows to the old, weathered door that hung unevenly on its rusted hinges.

Stop thinking and go.

Without looking down, he stepped off the curb and into a small stream of rainwater carrying gum wrappers, leaves, and cigarette butts to the storm drain at the end of the block. Shaking his now-soaked foot, he stepped out of the steady rivulet of water running through the gutter.

For a moment, he was just a kid again, without cares, bouncing through puddles after a rain. The smile on his face fled quickly, though, when he raised his eyes to peer again at the miserable-looking building in front of him.

As fear surged inside him and the knot grew in his throat, Leo continued across the damp street. It had been raining most of the day, and the smell of the rain still lingered in the chilly evening. His nose and ears were chilled in the cool evening. He sniffled.

Leo looked down the street about half a block at the solitary streetlight. The stars and that lonely light were all that fought against the oppressive feeling of darkness that assaulted him.

Leo paused in the middle of the street and stared up at the building. *It looks darker than it did from the other side of the street.* He questioned his own thoughts. *What am I doing here? Why would someone take Blaine into that old building? Who would take him in there? Are these just crazy thoughts?*

Leo pondered the questions that troubled his mind. He shrugged at his doubt and shivered in the cold, damp air. He straightened his back and clinched his fists to fight his fears and ward off the chill. He willed himself to take the next step and then the next.

Just steps from the sidewalk, his doubts stirred once more. *What if someone is trying to get me inside? Am I just being stupid and walking into a trap?*

Leo stepped over the raised and broken portion of the sidewalk, where a root had long ago cracked the concrete in search of moisture. He shuddered.

As he assessed the steps of the small porch, he sensed that something was familiar about this building. *Have I been here before?* He had an odd feeling of déjà vu.

He looked once more at the small porch that surrounded the door. It was made of just three wooden, rain-soaked steps that led to the front door. A weak-looking handrail to the right side leaned a bit toward him. He thought if he grabbed it, part of it might come off in his hand, so he eased his way up the steps without the use of the railing.

Leo took in the strong smell of mildew that came from the weathered wood of the porch and doorway. He had to duck his head in order to miss one of the many spider webs that were thick in the overhang above his head.

He stretched his left hand out to the handle of the door and paused. His heart raced. *Get ready, Leo. You don't know what's on the other side.*

He drew in a deep breath to still his heart; grabbed the old, English-style door handle; and turned the knob. He wasn't surprised that it turned and the door opened.

He pulled the door open a few inches and paused. The weary door hinges didn't easily give in to his tug. He glanced at a door knocker he hadn't noticed before. It was made of chiseled, rounded stone. It had three letters carved in the middle that spelled the word *sod.*

Sod? he thought. *What an odd thing to have on a front door.*

He opened the door wide and stepped in.

The smell of rain was immediately gone, and his senses were assaulted as he stepped into the entryway of the building. Leo noticed the odor of smoke, sulfur, and a mustiness that must have come from an ash-filled fireplace now damp with rain. His eyes strained to adjust to the near-darkness that contrasted with the star-filled night outside.

The stench of the air was repulsive, but the crushing feeling upon his chest had grabbed all his attention. He was struggling to breathe as he bent over in pain from the weight upon his chest. Some rescue this would be. He could barely breathe; how would he find and rescue his brother?

He would, though. He must; if his brother was in this building, he would find him. With his hands on his knees, Leo steadied himself and slowly regained his breath. When his breath returned, he stood up straight again to check out his surroundings.

Leo stood in a small foyer that led immediately into a long, dark hallway. He couldn't see to the end of the hall. His eyes were slow to adjust in the dim light, but he was breathing easier now. The pressure on his chest eased. With his courage wavering, he again clenched his fists, stiffened his back, and prepared to find Blaine.

Then Leo saw something move down the hallway.

It was quick, but he thought he saw a person pass through a doorway.

Leo tried to steady his shaky confidence. He cautiously walked toward the opening where he'd seen the person come out. He kept his eyes and ears alert to any possibility of danger. He couldn't afford to be surprised by a sudden attack. Whoever had Blaine might expect that he would come looking for him.

He crept along the hallway in silence. He kept himself against the wall to the right, hoping to blend in and go unnoticed by any others who might unexpectedly appear. He approached the opening where he thought the person had come from.

Leo cautiously came around the corner and prepared to enter the small room. He slowly pushed on the door. In the old, musty building, he expected the hinge on the door to creak. He was glad when it didn't. There was no one in the room, and there was nothing in it—nothing at all. There were no pieces of furniture. There were no chairs, tables, lamps, or even pictures. It was a completely empty room. There weren't even any lights; yet he could see clear enough to make out the empty details of the room.

Something about the light troubled him.

Leo stepped back out of the room and headed farther down the hallway. His search took him past four more empty rooms. He carefully peeked around the doors of each opening he came to. He saw the same thing: nothing. The rooms were completely empty.

What is it? Something nagged at Leo's thoughts

After the fourth room, Leo realized what had baffled him earlier. There were no lights in the rooms or in the hallway, but there was a smoky haze in the air throughout the hall and rooms. The smoke had a misty glow to it. He hadn't realized it until now. His eyes first needed to adjust to the darkness, but then he realized the eerie, hazy smoke was glowing.

As Leo puzzled about this, the heaviness suddenly returned to his chest and lungs and stole his breath away. It was stronger this time and brought him to one knee. Though he struggled mightily just to draw in a weak breath, he was careful to keep his head up. He fought against the oppressive feeling that engulfed his whole body.

A few seconds passed, and his breaths became fuller. The pressure on his chest eased, and his breathing slowly returned to normal.

What is causing these breathing struggles? Leo tried to control his feeling of panic. Beads of sweat dotted his forehead, so he wiped at his brow with his forearm. He stared at his moist palms, and though he was breathing better, he felt his muscles give way a little as he questioned whether he would have the strength to put up a fight for his brother if he had to.

He tried to come to grips with his thoughts when a huge scuffle erupted in the hallway. It sounded like a huge wrestling match was coming down the hallway. It sounded like feet and bodies slamming and scrapping against the floor and walls of the hall. Leo feared he would be discovered.

He edged toward the entrance of the room to hide behind the doorway. He listened as the sound of many feet shuffled past the open doorway. Leo peered through the crack between the door and the casing. He could see a mob of men wrestling with someone as they forced him down the hall.

"Keep a hold of him, and keep him quiet!" A strong voice barked orders to the men as they tried to control the man who obviously was struggling to resist their efforts. *Who did they have?*

Leo looked more closely and saw it wasn't a man they struggled with. It was a boy. The boy had blond, shaggy hair and a slender build.

It was his brother. Blaine was very athletic and often chosen first when friends were choosing sides to form a football or baseball team in the neighborhood. Blaine and Leo were two of the most athletic of the many kids on their street. They were often found in the thick of things when teams were chosen for anything from tackle football to army in the field or baseball on the school's ball field.

Even though there were several men, Leo could see how much they struggled with Blaine's athletic and wiry frame. A sense of pride caused the corner of Leo's mouth to turn up and unveil a small grin. Even though he was young, Blaine's sinewy strength gave this group of men more than they wanted.

As they struggled with Blaine in their clutches, they were clearly in view, moving past the opening of the room. They were all dressed in black and wore tight-fitting, long-sleeved shirts and pants. They all wore a patch on their right sleeve. On each patch were three letters. It spelled out *sod,* just like Leo had seen on the front door.

Is that a word, or are they initials for who these people are? The menacing look of the dark-clothed men fit well with the eerie, glowing mist of the dark building.

As his mind toiled over these thoughts, Leo realized he needed to make a decision about what to do with the mob that had his brother. *I should have brought my Bowie and bow.* With his bow and knife, he would have a better chance with these numbers. *How am I supposed to overcome these men with my bare hands?* He was just a youth and he had come to the battle without any weapons.

I can't overwhelm them all plus drag my brother out, too. There might be fifteen or sixteen men there. I'll let them pass and follow from a distance. As the mob scuffled down the hall, Leo tried to sneak out of the room in hopes of following in secret. It was a foolish move, and he was immediately noticed by one of the men in the back of the scrum.

"Hey!" The man alerted the group. Leo took off running toward the front door. He ran hard, but his lungs screamed in pain as they again struggled to provide him oxygen. As he struggled to stay ahead of the pack, he realized something had gone wrong. The hallway seemed too long! *Where is the front door I just came through?* he puzzled as he frantically looked for escape. *This is the same hallway, but it is too long! What happened? How could I have missed that doorway?*

Leo tried to keep running hard despite the puzzle of the missing door. The harder he ran, the more his legs felt like mush. He tried to run hard but felt stuck in slow motion. He desperately urged his legs to go faster, but they just wouldn't respond.

He was in a hopelessly long hallway. Everything seemed wrong and slow. The choking feeling in his lungs returned. Leo struggled to breathe and run but wasn't very successful at either. His pursuers were drawing close, and he feared he would soon be caught.

His heart raced as he heard the crush of men fast approaching. He tried to dart down another hallway, since the one he was in was hopelessly long. His quick turn down an adjoining hallway was a mistake. The floor immediately gave out beneath him, and he was unexpectedly in a free-fall.

He spun himself around, trying to catch something to stop his fall. When Leo turned, he was stunned to be staring into the frightening face of an enormous giant of a man. He instinctively opened his mouth wide to scream, but all that came out was silence. The sight of the huge man caused Leo to pull back his arms and take his chances with the fall into darkness.

Leo came to an abrupt stop. *Where am I?* He rolled over and pushed himself up to his knees, turned his head, and wondered what he was doing on his bedroom floor. "Oh, man, not again. That dream was so real!" Leo quietly mumbled to himself.

"What are you doing?" Blaine asked, looking down at Leo from the top bunk. His messy blond hair and freckles gave him a different look than his younger brother. They were both similar in build, but Leo was a little shorter. The girls all thought Leo was cute, but he was so shy that he hardly ever spoke to them—except Amanda. She was different. Leo and Amanda had a special friendship.

Blaine was a good-looking young boy, but he was the goofy type—always joking and playing pranks on his friends and younger brother. He was the free-spirited type who was comfortable talking with anybody.

"I fell out of bed," Leo proclaimed. "I had another weird dream." *It was more than weird,* he thought. *It was too real. Who or what was that huge man?*

"Well, since you're there, I'll use you to get down." Blaine stepped down from the top bunk, using Leo's back as a step stool. "It's time to get ready for school, Leo. Let's go."

"I'm coming; I'm coming." Leo hollered as he followed his brother down the hall. "Do we have any cereal yet? I'm getting tired of toast."

"Nope, it's toast or nothing. Mom didn't shop yet, but you better be quiet or she'll wake up and take the belt to you."

CHAPTER TWO

Toast for Breakfast

The boys stumbled sleepily down the hallway. Leo peeled off into the restroom and called to Blaine as he headed to the kitchen. "Hey, Blaine, can you stick a couple slices in the toaster for me too?"

"Yeah, no problem."

When Leo came out of the bathroom, his brother had a question for him. "Hey, what the heck was going on with you this morning?"

"What do you mean, Blaine?"

"I mean with the wrestling or whatever you were doing this morning in bed. You woke me up with all the tossing around you were doing. You said that was a dream?"

"Yeah, it was kind of weird; I don't know what was going on."

"You woke me up and practically shook me off the top bunk, bro!"

"Well, it was kind of weird, like I said, and you know how dreams are—crazy things happen, and you're not sure what went on after you wake up."

"Well, next time try to keep it quiet, huh?" From the kitchen window Blaine could see some of the neighbors preparing for school and work.

The boys lived in a clean, low-income neighborhood where the families looked out for each other and most of the kids on the block knew each other pretty well. There were about twenty or so kids living on the small Cul-de-sac at any one time. The street they lived on, named Lakeside Drive was in the small suburban town of Montoya.

Many of the homes in the area were those of military families. That meant there would always come a time for some family to move away. When that happened, the whole family would just pack up and leave. The kids got used to meeting and making good friends and then having to say good-bye and never seeing them again. It never felt right, but that was how life was for the kids on Lakeside Drive.

Most of the kids on the street got along really well. The kids thought the name of their street was funny, though, because there wasn't a lake for miles around. They walked, ran, played, and rode their bikes all over the little town of Montoya and never came across anything that looked like a lake. After a good rain during the spring, there were often good-sized puddles the kids would wade around in, but never anything like a lake.

Though there wasn't a lake, there was a place down the street from Leo's house where most of the kids could be found playing after school or during the weekends. The kids called it the dirt lot. It consisted of several acres of undeveloped land filled with trees, rocks, bushes, and clusters of decades-old oak trees that the boys and girls were often found climbing through the branches of. Out in the dirt lot, many make-believe army battles had been fought between friends. Rocks and sticks were usually the weapons of choice. The rock fights often ended with some kid getting blasted in the head and running home with blood streaming down his face.

Leo and his friends weren't the type of kids to ever purposely get into trouble, but being kids, they did occasionally get into some. Blaine and Leo would often laugh about one of the funnier things they almost got in big trouble for—tossing newspapers at the cars that drove by on Tenth Street.

Frank's younger brother, Louis, had an idea. Frank, one of the older kids on the block, had a paper route, and there were often a few papers left over each day. "We are not going to toss my papers at cars, Louis; you trying to get me in trouble?" Frank said.

After a little more protesting, Frank, finally agreed. That spurred several of the kids to rustle up some warm jackets, and then they were off with armfuls of ammunition to toss.

The boys thought it was great fun hiding in the bushes alongside the road and seeing who could get the best shot at the cars that zoomed past. They rarely hit any cars but had lots of fun trying. When they did hit a car, the papers would flutter, break apart, and scatter over the street. Drivers in the cars would point fingers and return angry looks, but the fluttering newspapers caused no harm, so they usually continued on their way.

The kids got the biggest kick from the faces of the people trying to yell at them. The boys had exhausted most of their papers when one driver ruined the whole thing by stopping. The driver decided to chase down the troublemaking kids, and teach them a lesson. He never did catch any of the boys, and the chase just added some adventure to the night and gave them a few more things to laugh about.

When they were done, Frank gave Louis and his friends a scolding and said he wasn't going to let them use his papers like that anymore. Louis then did what the others were thinking about doing. He grabbed one of the remaining newspaper rolls and tossed it at Frank. He hit Frank square in the face, and for the next half hour, the kids had a good-natured brawl.

They all laughed as they beat each other over the heads with paper weapons. In the end, their hands and faces were covered in newsprint ink, and shreds of paper were scattered all over Frank and Louis's front yard, where the donnybrook took place.

The boys loved the weekend nights and the innocent fun they brought after five days of going to school and getting homework done. The boys and girls on Lakeside Drive all loved to play. They were often out late at night when schoolwork didn't keep them in.

There weren't a lot of girls who played with the boys, but the few who did, fit in great and were seldom made fun of. The only qualifications for this club of kids were things like tossing footballs, shooting basketballs, and swinging baseball bats. School was just a necessary interruption in the constant playtime the kids on the street seemed to always be involved in.

Leo and Blaine were often out the latest, because their mother was very seldom home. She usually came home from her job at the nursing home in the early afternoon. She was often in a bad mood, and after a few hours of sleeping on the couch, she would get herself ready for a night out with her friends. Before she left in the early evening, she would write a couple notes for the boys. The notes were often about what chores to do, how to fix dinner, or what time they should be in bed.

Things had been that way for years, and Leo and Blaine had gotten used to taking care of themselves. They didn't know where their mother went at night, but her anger was often stirred by her drinking. The boys assumed she went out to do more of that with her friends.

Another typical morning was starting for the boys, as Blaine switched from staring out the window to the bread he was monitoring in the toaster.

The toast had popped, and now that Leo had his shoes on, he grabbed some butter out of the fridge and started spreading it on thick.

"Hey, save some butter for the poor kids down the street!" said Blaine.

"Yeah, sure, Blaine. We are the poor kids down the street, remember?" Leo countered.

"Yeah, well, can you save some butter for this poor kid?"

"There's plenty of butter, Blaine. I just like to cover the whole slice so it's nice and buttery."

The two brothers grew up like many kids who had divorced parents. They only saw their dad a couple times each year. He sent monthly child support checks, but there was never enough money for a lot of nice things. The boys figured their mother's income at the nursing home didn't leave a lot for cereal, doughnuts, or Pop Tarts for breakfast. They knew they didn't have a lot of things, but they didn't care all that much. Most of the families in the area weren't much for nice things anyway.

Having a little extra butter for his bread was luxury enough for Leo. He sprinkled on a thin layer of sugar to finish off the breakfast masterpiece. He loved sugared toast, even though he and his brother had spent the last couple weeks without anything but toast and milk in the morning. He was happy about having real milk that morning. "I'm glad we don't have that powdered milk."

"I know; that stuff is nasty, huh?" Blaine scrunched his face up in disgust at the thought.

Sinking in his teeth into his toast, Leo declared, "Man, I sure can cook!"

"I cooked it! You just put the butter on. Besides, I thought you were tired of toast!"

"I am, but it still tastes good." Leo licked the back of his fingers to capture the sugary butter that ran down the back of his hand. *"Mm, mm, mm,* that's good!"

"Well, move over, and let me get at some of that sugar, you dream-shaker." Blaine worked his way to the counter. The sink was full of dishes and had the smell of food that was several days old. He ripped off a paper towel and placed it on the counter where the least amount of old crumbs and jelly was.

"Dream-shaker?" Leo asked, puzzled.

"Yeah, I said dream-shaker. You head off into your crazy dreams, and I end up getting all shook up when you wrestle with your gremlins or whoever you're dreaming about."

"Sorry, I can't help it."

"Hey, look who's coming!" From his place behind the counter, Blaine could spy out the window and see Amanda coming up the driveway. "Is Amanda your girlfriend, Leo?'

"No, she's just a friend! I told her she could walk with us to school."

"I'll go let her in," Leo told Blaine. "You can finish sugaring your toast."

Leo was excited to see Amanda so early in the morning. His heart beat a little faster as he reached to open the door for her. He always looked forward to seeing her at school. She was a fifth-grader like him, and sat next to him in class. She had beautiful, long brown hair, twinkly eyes, and an easy smile. Leo thought she was the most beautiful girl in the whole school. He was too shy to ever tell her that, but because she was athletic and enjoyed playing sports with him and the other kids on the block, Leo could enjoy her company and her pretty face without saying anything.

Amanda took a liking to Leo's quiet nature, and the two of them were best of friends. Both of them loved to read, so they also spent a good amount of time at the library together.

Before Leo had a chance to open the door, he was surprised to see something hanging on it. "What is this, Blaine?" Leo couldn't believe what he saw. It was the same weird ornament he saw hanging on the front door of the dark building in his dream. Engraved in the middle of it were the same three letters in his dream—*s-o-d.*

"Huh, that's weird!" Blaine said as he leaned away from the counter to see what Leo was pointing at. "I don't know; it's probably something

Mom brought home last night. Some guy probably gave it to her. I'm thinking you should let Amanda in, though."

Leo opened the door, and unlike in his dream, he was met by the pleasant smell of Amanda and the twinkle of her eyes. *What makes her eyes twinkle like that?* he thought as he smiled at his friend.

As usual, Amanda had a sweet, flowery aroma that she probably sprayed on herself each morning. Leo didn't understand why girls sprayed themselves with perfume, but he always enjoyed the sweet aroma of Amanda.

"Hi, Leo, are you okay? You look like you've seen a ghost or something."

"Hi, Amanda. Oh, it's just this thing on our door. I've never seen it until right now! Check this out."

Amanda stepped in to take a peek. "Oh, what is that thing? Does that say *sod*?"

"I guess so. We don't know where it came from. Blaine thinks our mom must have put it on the door. Did you hear her come home last night, Blaine?" Leo asked.

"No, I was asleep, but let's go, guys. We got to get to school now. We can look at creepy ornaments when we get back."

The boys grabbed their lunches, books, and the remnants of their sugar toast and headed out the door. Blaine locked the door behind them. He was the older brother by just one year, so he had the responsibility of keeping the key safe.

CHAPTER THREE

Black-clad, Tall, and Staring!

"Eric, throw it!" Blaine ran open across the middle of the field, with Louis chasing after him. Eric let the ball fly. Blaine had to slow down a bit to catch the football, and when he did, Louis ran into his back and knocked him to the ground. Blaine still made a great catch, though.

"Ha-ha! Nice throw, Eric," Blaine yelled. "Its first down, guys. We're gonna score next time for sure."

"We are a beast! We can't be stopped!" Blaine loved to boast, and he was pouring it on.

Eric, Blaine, and Leo were having some fun with their latest scoring drive and started to strut and boast, but it was all good fun. This type of playful jesting was part of what the guys really enjoyed about the sports they played with each other.

"Yeah, that was a good catch, but bring it my way again, and I'll be running the other way with it for a score." Louis trash talked right back at Blaine.

The guys lined up for another play. They were playing three-on-three, because not everyone could come out to play. Eric was ready to take the snap for another play. He came up behind the pretend center, held the ball out, and called out signals like the real players in the NFL would do. "Ready-set! Red dog, four! Hike, hike, hike!"

The third hike was the signal. Blaine shot off the line on the third hike. He was lined up on the left of Eric, sprinted down five yards, and made a quick dash toward the middle of the field.

Leo lined up on the right side, sprinted in a straight line up the field, and headed toward the end zone. As he got to the broken fencepost that marked the end zone, he planted his right foot and cut back hard toward the middle. He had a sure touchdown if Eric caught sight of him. "Eric!" Leo gave a shout to get his attention, but the ball was already on its way.

"You got it, Leo!" Blaine yelled as his brother raced to where the ball had been thrown. Leo ran hard, and without having to slow down, he reached out to grab the ball that had been placed perfectly in front of him.

It was a sweetly tossed ball, and Leo made the easy catch to score another touchdown for his team. The brothers were winning, as they often did in these games. Sometimes Leo and Blaine joked that being on the same team was an unfair advantage. That day, they also had Eric, who all the kids knew was a special athlete.

"Okay, Louis. Take a walk, buddy. You know the rules—losers walk, winners talk!" Leo was quiet most of the time, but while out on the ball field, he enjoyed joking around and often seemed out of character with his boisterous jesting.

"Okay, quiet, man. Talk all you want. Just kick it to us; it's our turn to score now." Louis wasn't going to let his good friend get the last word in.

"Louis!" Louis's mother, Mrs. Hernandez, called out to him from down the street. It always amazed the kids how loud Louis's mother was. She expected an immediate response, and Louis was usually quick to reply.

"Oh, man," Louis mumbled softly to himself, but he knew he had to answer his mother's call. "Yes, Mom?"

"You need to get home right now. Your father's coming home soon, and you need to get the lawn done."

What a powerful voice, Leo thought.

"Okay, Mom!" Louis turned to his friends. "Sorry, guys. I gotta go. I'm supposed to mow the grass today. I better at least be mowing that grass while my Dad is pulling up, or I'll be in big trouble."

"Hey, no problem, Louis!" Blaine shouted at him. "It's like Leo said—losers walk, and winners get to stay and talk!"

"Oh, man, that's cold. I'll see you guys later."

"We'll see you later, Louis," Leo called out.

"Later, quiet man. Say hi to Amanda for me." At that Louis, jogged home to drag the old push mower out from beside his house.

"I will." Leo liked that people knew he and Amanda were such good friends, but he also knew his brother liked to make fun of him, so he made sure not to look over at Blaine right then. Blaine and the others did like having Amanda around, because she was as fast as most of them, and speed was always a good teammate.

"Leo, we should get home, too. Mom's probably left a note for us at home. We probably have some chores to do, too."

"Yeah, I know I got bathrooms this week again," Leo responded.

"Great! That means I don't have to be so careful when I aim. When I miss, I know my little brother will clean it up for me. *Wahoo!* It's another good day. We won at football, and I can make a mess around the toilet! Life doesn't get better than that, you know!"

"Miss too much, and I'll shake you off the bed again tonight."

"Okay, dreamer. I'll try to be careful."

The boys said good bye to Eric, Ralphy, and Lane as they all headed toward home.

On the way through the field, Leo and Blaine didn't notice the large group of teens who were fast approaching from the rear. As the teens approached, the crunching of their footsteps on the gravel finally caught the boys' attention. They stopped and turned to see who was coming.

There looked to be about fifteen or so teens—mostly boys, and all dressed in tight-fitting dark clothes. They all had very serious looks on their faces. Leo and Blaine thought it would be best to step off the dirt path and let the large, menacing group of kids pass by.

Leo got a cold chill as he got a better glimpse of the teens. They all had the same patch on their right arm that the men in his dream had the other night. It was the same three letters—*s-o-d.*

Leo was shocked to see people from his dream walking past him while he was wide awake. He reached out, grabbed Blaine's forearm, and squeezed it hard. Blaine winced but didn't take his eyes off the intimidating troupe as they passed by. Most of them had dark, evil-looking tattoos on the skin that wasn't covered up by their dark clothes. They had body piercings on their eyebrows, lips, and ears, and a couple of them had little chains connecting some of their piercings to other parts of their body. Blaine and Leo were freaked out by the teens, but they tried to keep from showing how nervous they felt.

"Good idea to get out of our way, little boys," one of the teens in the front said as he glared at the brothers.

Blaine and Leo did not dare say a word.

One of the teens in the center of the group was much taller than the others. He looked to be several inches past six feet tall.

Men dressed in black with sod *written on their sleeves and a huge man with them.* Leo recalled the similarity to his dream as the teens walked past. *These are just big kids, but that tall kid isn't a huge, ugly man like in my dream . . . but he sure is tall.* Leo puzzled over this as he looked from kid to kid to see if anything else caught his eye. When he looked back at the big kid, he was suddenly aware that the whole group of teens had come to a stop, and they all were staring at him. The tall kid gave a disturbing nod at Leo, and they all started walking again.

That guy stopped and stared right at me . . . they all did. Leo wanted desperately to just turn and sprint as fast as he could in the opposite direction. He guessed he had the speed to get away from these teens if they decided to give chase, but he was frozen at the moment and was hoping they would continue on their way.

Blaine and Leo silently stared as the teens got farther away. Blaine was the first to blurt out, "Oh, man! What was that all about? Did you see that monstrous guy staring at you?"

"How could I not?" Leo's words spilled out.

"He looked at you like he knew you—did he?"

"Um, I sure hope not."

"I didn't want to say anything while they were here, but you were squeezing the heck out of my arm, Leo. What was your problem?" asked Blaine.

"They were dressed like some of the people in one of my dreams, Blaine!"

"What?"

"Remember that bad dream I had recently?"

"Yeah," Blaine answered.

"You asked what it was about," Leo said, "and I really didn't know what to say."

"Oh, yeah. You said you saw weird stuff, or something—but what's that got to do with those kids?"

"Okay—this is, like, the weirdest thing ever, but in my dream, I saw a bunch of men dressed just like those teenagers. They had clothes just like them."

"Well, they just had black clothes on—lots of teenagers do," Blaine said.

"I know—but listen, Blaine. I know this sounds crazy, but sometimes you have dreams, and things are weird, and it's no big deal, 'cause it's a dream—no problem," Leo tried to explain.

"Okay, so in your dream, people dress like teenagers. What's the big deal?"

"Did you see those letters on that patch they were wearing on their right sleeve?" Leo asked.

"I didn't notice." Blaine rubbed at the indentations Leo's fingernails had made on his arm. "What about it?" He said, not bothering to look up.

"In my dream, it was the same three letters," Leo replied.

"Really?" Blaine started to get interested.

"Yes, really—and you know what else?"

"More weird stuff, right?"

"That label on their sleeves—it has the same three letters as the thing on our door at home."

"No way! What are the letters again?" asked Blaine.

"Not making it up, man—it's the same one, and I'm getting a little freaked out. The letters are *s, o,* and *d.* And you know what else?"

"Wait, the letters spell *sod,* like dirt and grass—that kind of sod?"

"Yes, it spells *sod,* but I doubt that it's talking about grass and dirt."

"I bet they're just a bunch of gardeners, Leo," Blaine joked.

"Did they look like gardeners to you, Blaine?"

Blaine shook his head.

Leo continued, "Also, at the end of my dream, just before I woke up on the floor, I was falling, and I reached back to try to grab onto something. I turned back in my dream to get a hold of something, and there was this huge, freaky-looking giant of a man staring right in my face!"

"Really—just like that big teenager was staring at you?"

"Not the same, no; in my dream, the giant was really angry and ugly and staring at me like he wanted to kill me or something."

"A giant?" Blaine asked with a small trace of a smile sneaking onto his face.

"Yes, a giant," Leo said. "That was the end of the dream. That's when I woke you up, I guess."

"Okay, I guess we should ask Mom if she's been dating any really large, ugly men lately."

"I know it just seems funny to you, Blaine, but that really is what I saw in my dream, and seeing that same patch on the sleeves of those teenagers and also in our own house—it just seems too weird. And then that guy is staring at me like he knew me or something. What do you think that was about?"

"I don't know. You're right. It does sound weird, but I'm not gonna go buy any magic beans to grow a beanstalk on the side of the house."

"Okay, make a joke, but you saw that guy."

"Yes, I did, and I think maybe you should get him to play on our basketball team. I think he could help," Blaine joked.

"All right, I can see you're not gonna be any help," said Leo.

CHAPTER FOUR

Amanda in Her First Fire Fight

Out in the dirt lot, the boys and Amanda hunkered down in a ditch. They peered past the trees into the fading light. The kids had chosen sides, and three of their friends had run off to hide. The after-dinner darkness was their favorite time to play army.

"Amanda, we need to be real quiet when we head out!" Blaine whispered. "Me and Leo will head the attack, but we need you to watch our backs in case we don't see them coming up behind us."

"What about a weapon for me?" Amanda was unarmed and wanted a weapon like Leo and Blaine had. The idea of a battle was new to her, but she was nervously excited at the idea of being in the middle of an attack. She liked the idea of attacking—it seemed better than just waiting and wondering when the enemy would strike and what the assault might look like.

"We'll just have to find you a weapon on the way. Don't worry about it; we will protect you for now. We'll find something for you to use," Blaine assured her. Amanda seemed fine with that answer.

Blaine was anxious to get the attack underway before he and Leo got flanked and were unprepared to mount a defense. Attacking was always better in Blaine's mind. Leo, like Blaine, was ready to go. He was ready for the attack.

Leo was quiet most of the time except when he gave an occasional exuberant shout after a great hit or catch on the ball field. At times like this, his quiet nature inspired him to think of the forest-dwelling Indians of the Old West days who could walk through thick forests without making a sound. Leo always tried to see how quiet he could be. He was always disappointed if he could hear his own steps. If he could hear himself, he knew the enemy might also hear, so he tried to be quieter.

"Which direction, Blaine?" Leo whispered into Blaine's left ear and stared out into the dark. The boys enjoyed playing army, and they really got into the fun of it.

"They headed over to the ridge there on the right," answered Blaine. "They're probably going to try to defend from there if they choose to set up a defensive position, so let's swing wide to the left. If they attack, they will probably come straight back from there, so we will be better off heading left anyway. It would take too long to swing all the way around, so I say left is the best choice for now."

"Then let's roll, bro. If we're real quiet, we might end up right on top of them before they know it."

"Amanda, we're moving! Keep low, keep moving, keep quiet, and look for any movement behind us or to our right—let's go!" Blaine enjoyed taking command of the battle, and he would always attack first if given the choice. Amanda smiled and complied with the commands for stealth.

Leo enjoyed being on the attack but saw the benefit in choosing the strongest defensible position. It was one of the differences between him and his brother. Leo thought it better to watch for the enemies' movements, and when possible, pick off the vulnerable if they got too close. A good attack could work, Leo thought, but more often, he preferred a well-defended position.

Leo's reading interests involved the wars, battles, and famous generals throughout history. He liked to read of the mistakes they made. The history books played out the lives of the past heroes and the many lives that were often lost by the selfish or foolish mistakes made by generals. Poor decisions by generals often led to needless deaths of soldiers. *Don't get us killed, Blaine,* Leo thought.

Leo liked to imagine himself as a wise general, making careful decisions that would save the lives of the men he led and bring a victory over the enemy. Leo thought he would be a great general, but being a shy quiet kid meant Blaine was usually in command, so once again, they were attacking the enemy.

On that Friday night, Eric, Frank, and Louis were the enemy. They had run off about ten minutes before to find a place to hide. Frank, the oldest, would call the shots for the other side. He would decide whether to attack or lay low and defend the high country.

Leo had asked Amanda to come along when they were at school. She heard him talking about playing army and she thought it sounded like fun. Leo felt funny about asking Amanda to join him but was thrilled when she said she would come along. Leo wouldn't say it, but he wanted to show off his skills of stealth to impress Amanda. Hopefully she would join them often.

With Blaine in the lead, the three of them snuck and slid their way toward the left. They stopped at all the big trees and lay still on the ground to peer around the trunk from both sides. Always, though, they kept their attention on their right. That's where Frank could bring a surprise attack. They tried their best to move in silence. Leo practiced his Indian-through-the-forest skills as they went.

"Leo!" Blaine stopped at another grouping of trees. He was leaning up against the twisted trunk of an old oak. He glanced back at Leo and Amanda with a look of concern.

"Do you see that?" Blaine asked. Leo and Amanda nodded their heads *yes.* About fifty yards ahead in a thicket of trees, someone had a large fire burning. They could just make out what looked to be a good-sized group of people around the fire. The fire looked large, as it gave off flashes, sparks, and occasional explosions of sap that sent glowing embers hurtling into the group of people.

"Is that them, Leo?" Amanda asked.

"No, I don't think so. Eric would never let the guys build a fire. Besides, they didn't have time to start a huge fire like that," Leo said.

"Plus, the guys took off in that direction over there," Blaine added as he pointed.

"Blaine, we should see how close we can get to it. Let's pretend it's an enemy army depot that holds weapons and ammunition." Leo's imagination and sense of adventure kicked in.

"You okay with that, Amanda?" Blaine checked with her first, because she was new to this battle adventure stuff.

"Yeah, I guess we can check it out, but we should be careful."

Amanda and the brothers had a new target, so they crawled, stooped, and slid on their bellies to get up as close as they could to see what this group of people was doing around this fire. They got right up to two big trees that were on the edge of a clearing where the group had the fire going.

The full moon shed plenty of light on the scene. The moonlight also cast many confusing shadows onto the dirt field. The three had to be careful not to be seen or not to accidently creep up on someone they didn't see in the shadows. The bright fire and the full moon caused enough confusion for the eyes that Blaine figured they could escape being seen as long as they stayed safely behind the row of trees that was just in front of them.

As all three of them settled into a position behind the trees, Leo and Blaine were surprised to see some familiar faces. They turned toward each other with knowing looks. They snickered and quietly giggled as they enjoyed the irony of being so close to the apparent secret meeting. The menacing-looking group of teenagers that passed by them the other day was in the middle of their dirt lot, having some kind of meeting.

"Don't make a sound, you two," Blaine whispered to his brother and Amanda. Leo and Amanda shook their heads as they eased down further in hopes of staying hidden.

CHAPTER FIVE

Hunted Down and Beaten with a Stick

"What do you think is going on?" Amanda looked scared as she whispered to Blaine.

"Not sure, but me and Leo have seen these guys before."

Leo gave Amanda and Blaine an anxious look as he held his finger up to his lips, imploring them to be quiet. They turned their attention to the bonfire meeting the teens were having in the field. Everyone in the midst of the gathering appeared to be a teenager. They were all wearing the same black clothing as the kids they crossed paths with earlier in the week.

Just like in my dream, but these are teenagers. In my dream, it was a bunch of men, and the giant—or whatever he was—was fully grown, they have the black clothing—same patch that spells sod. *Who are these people?* Leo thought about these things as he stared suspiciously at the group of teenagers gathered around the fire.

One of the teens wandered closer to where Leo was hiding. He moved aimlessly until he was less than ten feet away. He was mumbling something to himself and staring at the ground, not really interested in what the others were doing around the fire. He had an indifferent look on his face—or was it a scared look? He wasn't engaging with any of the other kids and looked like he wanted to be anywhere but where he was.

Maybe all these kids don't want to be here. Maybe they feel pressured to belong to this club or group, Leo guessed. The patches and the word *sod* had Leo stumped. He knew he should do some research on it when he got a chance. He would ask Amanda to help him with that. *She likes that kind of stuff.*

As the kids talked around the fire, Leo was able to get a good look at most of them. There were about twenty-five in all, and most of them were from the group that he and Blaine saw the other day.

Leo could feel the heat of the raging fire from where he hid. He saw one scraggly-looking, lanky kid sitting on a small rock upwind of the fire. Heavy clouds of black and white smoke billowed off in the opposite direction of where he sat. The smoke swirled among several of the kids and watered and irritated their eyes. Leo noticed several of them wiping at their eyes and dodging to escape the fickle winds that brought the smoke in their direction.

Leo could smell the smoke, the burning wood, and something else. An odd, unpleasant smell mixed with the smell of the fire. He surveyed the whole scene and picked out what he thought might be the source of the odd smell.

A little dish sat atop a small stump on the far side of the fire. In the middle of the plate sat a glowing, amber-red mound of burning ash. A small wisp of smoke rose up from the burning ash. Leo guessed it was incense of some kind.

Leo leaned over to Blaine and whispered in his ear. "This is weird! Did you see that incense plate they have over on the far side?"

Blaine said nothing but turned toward his brother with eyebrows high and eyes popping. He silently mouthed his response—*Wow!* As Leo read his brother's unspoken word, he felt something touch his hand. He instinctively yanked his hand in surprise.

The sudden movement caused a rustling of the leaves and gravel under his feet. The young teen who was close by glanced in the direction of the noise. He looked closely toward the trees where the three were in hiding. They held themselves stone-still and hoped they were well hidden by the shadows and trees.

The teen still looked scared. Seeing nothing in the shadows, he went back to mumbling to himself and looking disinterested.

Together, the three breathed a silent sigh of relief. Leo and Blaine looked at each other and then back at Amanda, who had startled Leo by trying to grab his hand.

Amanda's fingernails were in her teeth; she looked like she was about to chew off a couple. *I'm so sorry, Leo,* she mouthed in silence. In a barely audible whisper, she continued, "I'm scared, you guys. I don't like this." Leo waved to her to come closer and was surprised when she didn't just inch forward but grabbed a hold of his right arm with both hands and snuggled up to him. She rested her chin on his chest. She was hanging on tight.

This sent a chill of excitement through Leo. He had never had a girl so close to him before. He didn't know how to react to her hanging on so tight, but he liked the feeling. He froze and took care not to pull away, because he didn't want her to let go. He saw Blaine glance over at her arms wrapped tightly around his arm.

"Don't be freaking us out, Amanda," Blaine whispered. "If they hear us or see us, we are going to have to run like crazy. Can you run through this field in the dark if you have to?"

"I'm so sorry, Blaine," she whispered. "Yes, I can run; just don't leave me. This is kind of creepy, you guys."

Leo, still feeling the rush of having Amanda hanging on so tight, dared not move a muscle. He leaned toward her ear and caught the familiar whiff of her flowery perfume. "Let's try to see what they are doing, Amanda—but just stay still, and try not to make any noise," he said.

"Okay, Leo. Can I just hang on to you?"

"Yes." That's all he dared to say as he turned his head to look again at the teens and their meeting. Leo's mind and emotions raced. He tried to guess the connection to these teenagers and his dreams. He was still scared of the look on the face of the huge man in his dream. He wondered about the way the tall teen stared at him as though he knew him or could read his thoughts. Now Amanda was holding tightly to him in fear of the mystery teens who had popped out of his dreams.

Leo was euphorically happy to have Amanda hanging on his arm, but he was also sitting twenty or so feet away from real-life apparitions that had materialized out of his dreams. He didn't know whether to be freaked out by what he saw or just happy to be sitting there with Amanda. He tried to focus his straying thoughts on the teens in the clearing in front of him.

Back at the fire, there was the expected popping of wood logs as their sap and air pockets met with the heat of the fire. Along with the popping sounds came the tiny explosions of embers flying into the night. The lanky kid was still poking at the fire with a long stick. Leo watched as he picked up a log from a large pile at his side and tossed it onto the blazing fire.

When the log landed on the top of the fire, it sent many more sparks up into the sky. It also loosened the logs below it. The weight of the new log sent the other logs tumbling. The whole fire shifted and sent a sizzling stream of sparks flying into the night sky. The teens turned toward the disturbance.

"Whoa! Did you guys see that?" The lanky fire-watcher liked the attention his fire was getting.

"Craze, be careful! We are not here to let you burn the field down. The fire is big enough already. We need to put it out when we leave, so that's enough!"

"All right; just calm down. I got it." The boy, Craze, seemed to be just as disinterested in the meeting as the scared teen who was wandering off. He looked to be satisfied just playing with the fire. He probably would have been just fine burning the field down after they were done, too. Maybe his likely addiction to fire was how he got his nickname.

"Quiet, everyone. He's coming!" The kid who yelled at Craze hollered out a word of warning to the whole crowd.

With the warning, two teens stepped out from the trees just in front of the stump that held the plate of burning incense. They each had a dark red sash draped over their right shoulder. The sashes hung around their hips like those in a beauty contest. There were lots of strange symbols emblazoned on the sashes. Along the bottom of the collection of symbols were the familiar letters that spelled the word *sod.* They each held what looked like a curled horn from a ram.

"Sons of Darkness, come to attention!" The one who had barked orders at Craze called all in the clearing to pay attention. At his call, everyone—even the young, scared kid—turned and bunched up closer to the two kids with the animal horns.

Did he say Sons of Darkness? Leo thought. *Who would want to be called that?*

The bunched-up crowd obstructed the view of the kids from where they hid, but they were able to relax a bit as the teens pushed farther away from where they sat.

Amanda still clung tightly to Leo's arm, but she looked less tense.

"That's better. I like them farther away like that," Blaine said.

"I know," responded Leo. "That was a little close. I sure hope we are going to be able to run faster than all these guys." Leo voiced the fear he had about their chances of getting away when or if they had to run for it.

"Remember, you two need to help me get out of here, too." Amanda felt relieved that the group was farther away, but she also knew they should think about getting away unnoticed. "Do you guys have any idea who these guys are? You said you saw them before."

"It was over by the football field a few days ago," Blaine answered. "After playing a game with Eric and Louis, we were heading home, and some of these guys came walking by us. They gave us some evil stares and tried to intimidate us. I'm thinking they're not very nice guys."

"Where do you think the big guy is?" Leo asked.

"Waaahooooong!" Blaine and the others ducked their heads in surprise at the sudden sound of woeful horn-playing. They turned their heads toward the group of teens, where the sound was coming from. Out from the trees came the big guy they were wondering about. The two sash-wearing horn-blowers were hidden from their view, but the tall kid towered over all the others in the crowd and could be easily seen.

"Oh my!" Amanda couldn't help herself as the cry escaped out of her mouth before she thought to stop it. She was shocked at the height of the teen who stepped out from behind the trees. He rose at least a foot over many of the heads of the other teens in the gathering.

Despite the noise of the horns, some in the crowd turned angry faces toward the sound of Amanda's cry. "Lug, go see who that is!" The same guy who had spoken earlier was barking more orders. "And bring them to me!"

"Yes, sir. Chin, Stew-pot, come with me!" A person who must have been Lug called to a couple of others to come with him to see who was spying on the meeting.

These kids have funny names, Leo thought as he processed the names and the fact he needed to move fast.

"Leo, let's go now!" whispered Blaine. "Amanda, stay close, and watch your step; we are on the move." All three were instantly up and running.

Amanda was scared—and she looked it. The boys were also scared, but their faces showed determination as they cast aside all efforts at secrecy and bolted off in a sprint through the field.

Leo gave an assuring look to Amanda as he hung tight to her hand. The three of them ran in lockstep through the terrain. Their run was made more difficult by the moon-cast shadows that made it harder to see some of the obstacles on the path. The field, like any plot of earth, was uneven and rocky in some places, and the shadows completely hid many of the dips and stones in the darkness until they slammed a toe or knee into one.

"Hey, you little kids, when we catch you, you're dead!" one of the pursuers shouted in warning.

Leo glanced back to see if the three had put any distance between themselves and their chasers. He saw movement and a few guys stumbling through some of the bushes they had just run past. He held tighter to Amanda's hand. She was doing a great job of staying with him and his brother, who were used to running through this field. "Blaine, we can't lead them to our house. We shouldn't even let them know which street we live on."

"I know, Leo, but let's just get away first."

"Hey, guys!" The startled shout came from right in front of them.

"Whoa!" Blaine gave out a shout as all three were suddenly sent tumbling into somebody. They fell into a tangled mass of limbs.

"Leo, Blaine, it's us." Eric was trying to push them off him. "What are you running from?"

"Some big kids are chasing us. We got to go, Eric. They're right behind us!" Blaine shouted toward the pile where he heard Eric talking.

"How many are there, Blaine?" Frank, was big and strong and usually up for a fight. He was thinking of putting up a defense. Blaine blurted back, "I think maybe three, but there's, like, twenty of them back just a little ways."

Just then, their pursuers burst through the bushes and out of the darkness and were right on top of them. "Hey, you punks, you want to tell us what you were doing spying on us?" It was the one called Lug. He was stout, but his face looked gaunt, with pronounced cheekbones and deep-set eyes that seemed especially threatening as he approached. Leo recognized him as being one of the teens he crossed paths with after football the other day. His neck was plastered with tattoos that started high on his neck and disappeared under his shirt. He came up and stood near Leo and the others, who were still struggling to gain their feet after their fall.

This gave Lug the advantage he wanted. Lug stepped right up to the small pile of kids and stood over the four, looking menacingly down at them. As Lug stood over them, Frank stepped toward him from the side and tightened the grip on the stick he held. A half hour earlier, it was a pretend machine gun, but now it was a real weapon that he was willing to use against this teen called Lug.

Eric, Leo, and Blaine were studying their own predicament and looking for a way out.

Lug noticed Amanda. "You guys still playing with girls, huh? Maybe you might want to run home and dress up some dolls together—but before you do, I think I might just drag you back to see the Nephi. He will make you crap in your pants so bad. You will never want to come out of your house again!"

"What is a Nephi?" Leo spoke up. He was scared but also curious about who these kids were and what they were doing.

"The Nephi is your worst nightmare come true, kid."

Nightmare—I have those, Leo thought.

"Leo, don't talk to this guy. We're heading home anyway." Frank had stepped closer, and Eric was squirming his way out from under the pile he caused by running into Leo.

"So your name is Leo, huh? I think I will let the Nephi know that a kid named Leo is snooping around at the meeting. I think he will want to meet you, Leo. Bring your girlfriend, and let's see if you can keep from peeing in your pants. He's already not happy that you were here."

"We're not going to your barbeque or whatever you're having over there," Frank blurted out. Frank stood about a foot away from the taller teenager, but he was not planning to back down.

"Chin, break him!" Lug barked the order at one of the two boys who had given chase with him.

At the order, Frank ducked low to avoid the attempted push that came from behind by Chin. As Frank dipped below Chin's arms, he steadied himself on both knees, grabbed his stick in both hands like a baseball bat, and swung as hard as he could at the exposed left knee of Lug. He snapped the stick on the teen's knee. Pain shot through Lug, and he crumpled to the ground. The boy called Chin and the other one nicknamed Stew-pot lunged toward Frank.

Blaine, Leo, and Eric were quick to respond when they saw what Frank had done. Both Blaine and Leo exchanged a knowing glance before they launched into a head-first dive toward the exposed legs of the two on-rushers. Just like in the many sandlot football games they had played together, they took the two larger attackers down immediately. Louis eagerly jumped in and was already on top of the ailing Lug, pounding on his head. As Leo and Blaine took out Chin and Stew-pot, Eric helped Amanda to her feet and was quick to aid the others.

As Eric helped to keep down the foes Blaine and Leo had brought to a crumpled heap, he gave some frantic advice. "We have got to scramble out of here, guys. If there's a lot more of them, we need to get going."

"He's right." Blaine said. "Frank, are you good to go? We should run now!"

"Amanda! Are you ready? We have got to go—and now." Leo made sure Amanda knew he and the others would watch out for her.

At that, the kids were off and running through the darkened field, leaving the surprised teens in crumpled, moaning heaps on the ground.

CHAPTER SIX

The Shah

The kids burst onto the street that edged the field and started to run straight to their homes.

"Leo!" Blaine yelled to grab his attention.

"Yeah, Blaine?" Amanda had let go of Leo's hand and ran beside him. Everyone was pumping arms and legs to put as much distance as possible between themselves and their pursuers.

"We can't let them see where we live. We have to go someplace besides home," Blaine hollered to his brother.

"I do not want those creeps knowing where I live—that's for sure," Amanda said. She was feeling better now that they were out of the field but certainly not eager to lead them to where she lived.

At Blaine's advice, the kids made a quick detour, turned left, and headed up the street. They zipped past the streetlight on the corner of the street where they lived. As they ran, they looked behind anxiously to see if they had been followed. After seeing no one following, they all stopped under the next streetlight they came to.

Taking in deep breaths, they rested their hands on their knees. Finally, they all breathed a collective sigh of relief.

"Whew! That was what I call fun! Did you see me whack that dude?" Frank announced in gloating triumph.

"That was nice, Frank," his brother, Louis, said. "You sent him down in a heap. He's going to be slowed up a bit, I think, but he is going to be pretty mad if he catches up to you."

"I'll whack him again. I'm not afraid of those creeps. Let 'em come," Frank boasted. He jutted his chin out in defiance, just daring them to challenge him.

"Well, if there's just three of them, maybe, but not if there's twenty or more." Eric, the fastest of them all, knew he could probably outrun the older boys, but he also knew that Frank was sometimes too confident in his ability to fight his way out of trouble.

"It was great that we got away from those three, but we can't let the whole bunch of them find us and start trying to run us down." Eric, in his usually calm manner, tried to talk some reason into everyone.

"Yeah, you're right, Eric." Frank knew Eric was right, but he was still proud of taking the kid out with the stick to his knee.

"Well, how about me and my bro taking out the two who were ready to take you out, Frank?" Blaine added with a little boasting of his own. "We had your back, Frank."

"We got 'em good, didn't we, Leo?" Blaine traded a loud high-five with his brother.

Leo grinned and nodded. He was nervous as it happened, but now he was enjoying the memory of how easily he and his brother took down the two big kids.

Amanda jumped in. "Guys, we should get going. You can brag about it later, but they could still be coming for us."

"Good idea, Amanda. Don't you think we should get going, Blaine?" Leo wanted to take charge but always deferred to his brother.

"Yeah, let's go see the Shah," Blaine agreed.

"The Shah?" Amanda asked Leo.

"He's some old Iranian guy who owns the liquor store over by the market. Sometimes he lets us have some of the old Twinkies or doughnuts before he throws them out."

"Yum," Amanda sarcastically volunteered. "Let's hurry up before he throws them in the trash—or maybe we should just go through his trash can. I'll let you go first, Blaine."

"Amanda, if you're going to hang out with us, you're going to have to get used to eating old food and fighting your way out of the field once in a while." Blaine had a sly smirk on his face as he instructed his young female protégé.

"I see that now, but can we go before those guys see us standing here?"

With the decision made, they started off to the Shah's liquor store a few blocks away. It was getting close to 8:00, and everyone but Blaine and Leo would be expected back home soon, so it would have to be a quick diversion to throw off whoever might be following them.

The friends knew a lot of the families in the homes they passed along the way. Most of the houses had lights on in several of the rooms. Mothers were cleaning up after evening meals, and kids and dads were picking out shows to watch as they settled on couches with full stomachs. At a couple homes, people were already out on porch swings with newspapers and magazines in a favorite spot, ready to digest their meals under the cool evening sky. As the kids hurried past, they would wave or nod, returning gestures to the older people enjoying peaceful moments on their front porches.

With the help of streetlights, the full moon, and the many porch lights, the kids had plenty of light to show the way. Fortunately, there were no menacing dark alleyways to pass through or busy streets to cross. If not for the angry youths who were in pursuit, this would feel like any normal Friday night. The kids knew their neighborhood well, and most of the families knew and looked out for them.

Moths and bugs fluttered about, chasing after the lights. Leo watched the dance of the moths as they passed each house. It always mystified him when he would watch them. *Why were they so attracted to something that was so deadly to them? Couldn't they see their moth friends get fried? Couldn't they see how this dance would end? I bet those teenagers are as stupid as these moths, dancing around the fire like they did—and it will just lead to them getting in big trouble.*

How are my dreams coming to life like this? Leo thought more about the things that troubled him. *That dream of the dark building . . . Blaine being captured . . . those men . . . and that huge, fierce-looking giant.* It seemed his dreams weren't following the usual pattern of occurring after a familiar experience. *It's twisted now. I had the dream, and now I'm seeing some of it come true. What did that kid, Lug, say? "The Nephi is your worst nightmare." I hope it doesn't get any worse than this. Did that big kid somehow know about my dreams? Is that why he was staring at me?* Leo shuddered at the thought.

The group crossed the third crosswalk with the little strip mall in front of them. The Shah's store was near the end and to the right.

At the intersection, there were just a few cars. The kids waited for a clear path and darted across the street. Still being a little cautious, they were careful to look back to see if there was any sight of the three teenagers. No one looked to be following, so they started to feel better about their escape. The parking lot of the mini mall was busier than the street they had just run across. There were many cars parked in front of the numerous stores.

The kids passed a store clerk who was outside, picking up trash in the parking area in front of the Shah's liquor store. The lot reeked of oil, dirty pavement, and spoiled garbage in the overflowing trash cans. Trails of ants were busily traveling back and forth from their hole in the ground to an especially ripe trash can. Several cockroaches scurried through the discarded tin cans that never made it to the trash can.

Amanda took note of the overflowing can just outside the front door. “Hey, Blaine, there’s probably some nice Twinkies in there. Can you pick me out a couple?”

“Nice, Amanda, but I think I’ll ask the Shah for some first.”

“You guys, we need to be quick. Our parents will be expecting us home soon. It doesn’t look like those guys are following, so let’s see the Shah and then go.” Frank was tough around his friends, but that toughness came from the stern discipline he and Louis received from their father. He wasn’t an abusive parent, but he was clear on his rules, and he expected his boys to be home at a reasonable hour.

“Good idea, Frank. I gotta go, too. It’s getting late.” Eric said, he was anxious to get into the safety of his own home and be under the watchful eyes of his parents.

“We’ll just say hi to the Shah and then go. I think the coast is clear,” Blaine assured everyone.

Leo noticed just a few people among the several aisles of chips, sodas, beef jerky, and other snacks. He didn’t take much notice of who they were as the six friends made their way to the front counter, where they saw the Shah and his son waiting on a couple customers who had come in for some beer and chips.

The Shah was a friendly, brown-skinned man with a bright smile and wonder-filled eyes. He reminded Leo of someone in stories or movies who might be hiding a bottle with a magic genie in the back room. Since the Shah was of Persian decent and had the accent to go along with it, Leo could easily imagine him flying around on a carpet, holding a magic lamp. His name wasn’t the Shah; that was just what the boys and some of his American friends called him. He told the boys of his life in

Iran when the Shah of Iran was still in charge. He was very proud of his country, but the government had changed since he was there, and the people had become more oppressed and scared of their leaders. His stories of his life as a boy in Iran made Leo wish he could have shared some of the adventures with the Shah.

The Shah saw the boys approaching, and his face brightened. He liked the boys. The Shah had often told the kids that they reminded him of his days as a boy in Iran. He had many childhood friends whom he no longer got to see. “Ah, my little men! You are out late tonight. What can I get you?”

Blaine leaned over the counter and whispered the word that he hoped would get him a treat. “Twinkies?”

“Seeking golden treasures before they get thrown to the dumpster?” The Shah smiled at him and finished with a sly wink.

“That’s us, Shah—treasure hunters in the night. Cream-filled treasures will satisfy our desires tonight.” Blaine enjoyed the subtle give-and-take and went along with the Shah’s comparison of golden treasure.

The Shah was always happy to give the kids some of the pastries that were still good but could no longer be sold because the sell-by date had expired. He found it to be a good business practice, as he developed trust and steady clientele from the parents of the kids who would drop by as well.

“No school tomorrow for us, Shah, so we decided to visit you after dinner.” Eric put in.

“Is that right, Mr. Eric? It’s almost time for little men to be going to their homes, though, I suspect. Why do your parents let you stay out with the owls and the coyotes?”

“There are no coyotes out here,” Frank said.

“But there are, Mr. Frank, there are. The things of the night do not always show themselves to the little men, but they are there.” The boys gave him a puzzled look. They knew he meant more than what he just said, but he often spoke in riddles, and the kids rarely tried to figure out the meaning.

"We saw a few scary things out in the night already," Leo said.

"Ah, my little man, Leo, what things have you been seeing? Did you see the coyotes that Mr. Frank doesn't believe in?"

"No, we didn't see coyotes," Leo answered. "We just saw a bunch of teenagers having a bonfire in the field by our house."

"Is that right, my little man? I see that you have brought in a friend you have not introduced me to. How is it that such a beautiful little princess has chosen to be in the company of trash-hunters?"

"That's golden-treasure-hunters, not trash-hunters, Shah." Blaine wouldn't let the kindly Persian store owner get in that jab without a comeback.

"Oh, I'm sorry. Yes, you are hunters of golden treasure, aren't you? But you have surely found a treasure in this lovely young lady. Leo, what is your lovely friend's name?"

Leo was now a little embarrassed for the attention Amanda was getting and the idea that she was his special friend. "Her name is Amanda."

"Nice to meet you, Princess Amanda. You may call me Mr. Rajeev, but these treasure-hunter friends of yours know me as the Shah."

"It's nice to meet you Mr. Rajeev." Amanda responded back with a little curtsy because of all the royal attention Mr. Rajeev was giving her.

"Are you here to learn the skills of these late-night hunters—the little men who seek soft, golden treasures from the man of Persia?"

"No Mr. Rajeev, I'm not here for the Twinkies. I just like to be with these little men." She chuckled as she used Mr. Rajeev's title for her friends.

"They're nice little men," she added, and then she looked over at Leo and winked.

Leo smiled and felt his face flush with warmth. He looked down and spied a gum wrapper on the floor. He reached down, picked it up, and took it to a nearby trash can, trying to hide his blushing face from Amanda.

"Okay, Amanda. Don't you start with the little men stuff, too," Blaine interjected.

"It's cute, Blaine. Besides, you are little men." Amanda now was winking at Blaine, too, but he wasn't embarrassed like Leo—just a little annoyed. He thought Amanda was trying to make fun of him.

Frank cut in. "Hey, you guys, me and Louis gotta go, so maybe we'll see you tomorrow. You guys playing some football with us?"

"You bet. Don't forget, me and Leo still get Eric," Blaine said. "We will beat you again, so get ready for the losers' walk."

"Whatever, Blaine." Louis spoke up. "I think you're gonna be too full on Twinkies, and these speedy feet will just run right by you."

Frank and Louis traded hand slaps and high-fives and strutted out the door toward home.

As their two friends left, the final four of the Twinkie treasure-hunters turned their attention back to the Shah. They bantered back and forth a little more about things. The Shah's son started to join in on the fun, too. As they talked, Leo was suddenly chilled by the voice that spoke out from behind.

"Hey, Leo!" the voice yelled, "the Nephi still wants to see you!"

Leo turned around slowly; he knew who was behind him. It was Lug, and he didn't look very happy. Lug stared down at Leo, slowly walked around him, and stood next to Blaine. Leo noticed Lug was limping from the blow he received from Frank. As he stood next to Blaine, he rested his right forearm on Blaine's shoulder and leaned into him. Blaine looked troubled but held firm under the weight of the older boy.

Clung! The unexpected sound from the counter startled everyone. The Shah had slammed the handle of an aluminum baseball bat on the counter. "I see the coyotes have shown up now that Mr. Frank has gone." The Shah stared directly at Lug as he spoke. His usual friendly voice and smile were gone. His bat spoke loudly for him. It was a simple message to the threatening teens, and they appeared to understand.

"We just wanted to say hi to your little friends, sir," Lug said. "We meant no harm. We're going, but we wanted them to know that we know who they are and to tell them that our friends want to meet them, too." Lug was slow and direct in his delivery to the kids, but as he spoke, he never took his eyes off Leo. "The Nephi wants to see you, little boy." Lug dipped his eyebrows lower over his already squinted eyes. It gave him a more fearsome look.

Clung! Clung! The Shah banged his bat twice more on the counter. He was serious and was not about to let the punks threaten his young friends. "It's time for the coyotes to go now. Find some possums to chase out there in the night, if you must—but you need to go now and leave my friends alone. If you don't leave now, the police will be asking me why I have so many dents in my nice new bat." As he said this, he took the bat in both hands and rested it on his shoulder. His son, who had been watching everything, moved to the end of the counter and reached below it. He pulled out another baseball bat.

"We're leaving now, camel-lovers. Don't get all upset; we're just making friends." Lug dismissed the threat from the Shah with a wave, and he turned to walk out. Chin and Stew-pot followed him. Lug tried to hide his limp, but it was obvious his leg was still hurting.

A small smile crept onto Leo's face despite the scare he just had.

CHAPTER SEVEN

Druid Rites and Visions into the Fantastic

The smirk was still on Leo's face when Amanda turned to him. Now that the threat from the teenagers was gone, Amanda grabbed both of Leo's shoulders and shook him once. She looked him square in the face and tried her best to look mature. "Leo, who were those boys? Why were they looking at you like that? Why did they seem to be so mad at you, and who is this Nephi guy that wants to meet you? What are you doing hanging around with these older kids like that? I thought you didn't know who they were!" She took a flustered breath in the middle of her tirade. She was scared and didn't understand why the teenagers seemed to be directing their attention at Leo.

"I don't know who they are or who this Nephi is. I'm just as surprised as you are, Amanda. I think we should . . ." Leo paused. "I think we should do some research on this."

"Research! Your answer to this is research?" Amanda was surprised by Leo's calm response to her verbal explosion.

Leo looked at Blaine. "Blaine, I don't think I will be playing any football tomorrow. Me and Amanda might be going to the library." Turning back to Amanda, he asked, "You will go with me, won't you?"

"Of course I will—if you can help me understand why these kids you supposedly don't know seem to want to hurt you."

When Saturday morning came, Blaine got ready for football with his friends, but Leo still insisted that he was going to the library and not with his brother to play football. Blaine couldn't understand his brother's interest in books and the library. He thought Leo was crazy for wanting to go to the library and miss playing football on a Saturday. As Leo left for the library, Blaine yelled out the door, "You're crazy, Leo! Why don't you just come and play some ball with us? Forget about those guys. We will probably never see them again."

Leo stopped halfway down the brick walkway that led away from the front door. He thought about the weeds he saw starting to creep over the edge of the bricks. He knew that his mother would notice and that he better make time to do the yard work or he'd get another taste of her quick temper.

"I have to look up some stuff, Blaine. This is just too weird—all this stuff that's going on. These guys have come out of my dream, and now they act like they know me. You tell me if that's not weird."

"Are you sure, Leo? 'Cause sometimes we think we dream stuff, and then . . . I don't know. I don't know what I mean, but we're never going to see those kids again. Let's just go play some ball!"

"I already told Amanda I would meet her at the library."

"All right," Blaine responded, "but if Louis scores a touchdown today, it's your fault!"

"You tell Louis he better enjoy it, because I'll be back," Leo said.

—

Amanda and Leo were back in the city library, where they were used to spending time together. Both of them were good students, thirsty for knowledge, and regular visitors to the library. Their study habits made them favorites of their teachers and regular targets for their school friends. They were always well prepared for any pop quizzes or big tests, and the kids who sat next to them could often be found sneaking peeks at their papers when the teachers were distracted. They were only in fifth grade, but both put most high school students to shame with the research and study skills they had already acquired.

Just less than an hour after arriving at the library, Amanda and Leo had compiled stacks of books on the table in front of them. The librarian's assistant had helped them find many of them. The assistant had taken a special interest in helping them when she overheard them asking the lead librarian if she could help them find out about someone or something called a Nephi. Her aid was especially helpful, but Leo was suspiciously curious about her and why she took interest in their studies after hearing about the Nephi.

Leo and Amanda found many of the books in the religious section. Some of the books seemed a bit bizarre and occult-like, which made Amanda a little uncomfortable. She didn't think her parents would approve of her looking at some of them.

Amanda and her family were regular attendees at the Assembly of God Church on Elm Street. She really enjoyed going every Sunday and especially liked the Sunday school class. Her class was a mixture of third-, fourth-, and fifth-graders—about fifteen on most Sundays. She liked the games, crafts, and songs, but most of all, she enjoyed hearing the stories from the Bible. It fascinated her to hear the stories from a book about times and people from thousands of years ago. Amanda was daring and liked to hear adventure stories—especially those of a young boy named David who wrestled lions and bears and fought giants. Her teacher was a sweet old lady named Mrs. Borland. Mrs. Borland was careful to make sure everyone was welcome and loved when they came to her class. She often had homemade cookies or cupcakes for the children. Mrs. Borland was frail with age, and her dry, wrinkled hands sometimes trembled while she held the Bible in front of the children as she told the stories. Her tenderness with the children made a big impression on Amanda.

Amanda enjoyed her Sunday school class so much that she invited her friends to go with her at times. She had pestered Leo about coming with her, and he finally did go with her a few times. Just as Amanda had told him, he did enjoy the class and the cupcakes and games. The previous Sunday, Leo had attended again after missing many months. The elderly Mrs. Borland told the popular story of little David facing the giant.

Leo was short and often felt like he was living in a world of giants, so he could relate to the courage David had. He admired the confidence David had in his God and the strength it gave him to face the giant that nobody else was brave enough to face. Leo wanted to be that brave, too.

Amanda couldn't escape the similarity between the huge man Leo described seeing in his dream and the giant that young David faced in the story from the Bible. And now there was a tall teenager at the bonfire. The kids called him a Nephi for some reason. Was that teenager who towered over the other teens a young giant? Amanda knew it was a silly thought, but still she wondered. In stories about giants, dragons, and the knights who were set in battle with them, the giants were always full-grown. Surely they started out as being younger and smaller, Amanda imagined. Had Amanda seen a young giant last night at the bonfire?

Amanda's thoughts caused her to stray from the books in front of her. She rolled her head around a couple times to loosen her neck and stretched her arms high over her head. *"Aaaahhh!"* She exhaled and hollered to relieve the tension she felt from sitting and staring at books too long.

"Quiet, Amanda," Leo implored as he gave her a friendly but stern look.

"Sorry, I needed to stretch." Amanda looked around the library. In the corner of her eye, she noticed the librarian's assistant at the end of the table, appearing to stare at her and Leo. Amanda turned to look at her. The young girl, who looked to be just out of high school, suddenly turned her attention away from them and returned to restocking books on the shelf next to her. Her sudden movement made her previous inactivity more obvious.

"She's been watching us this whole time." Leo said to Amanda.

"I thought she was. Some of these books she brought are a little creepy. I don't think my parents would want me looking at this stuff, anyway." She picked through some of the books. "What are these books, Leo? *Dark Angels. Crossing Over Fire. Warped Angels. The Book of Winged Rebellions.* She expects us to read through this stuff?"

"I know; some of that stuff is weird, but we're not looking for instruction manuals on how to join some weird club. We're trying to see what those teenagers might be up to. Plus, I want to know why they were dressed like the people in my dream—and what is up with that patch with the word *sod* on it?"

"Well, let's crack open some more creepy books, then," Amanda said with a sigh. "I'm not looking at any of the real creepy stuff, though."

"Thanks, Amanda, and I'm sorry about the creepy books—but I'm really glad you're here to help me."

A couple more hours passed, and Leo and Amanda started to get hungry. They had sifted through most of the books that were set on the table in front of them. Amanda leafed through a book about ancient monuments and druid oracles.

One book, *Visions into the Fantastic,* grabbed Leo's attention, and he set it aside while he shuffled through the pages of the many other books. On the cover, a single red eye was set over a menagerie of various symbols and images. Among those images were rams' horns and an incense stand like they had seen at the fire gathering in the dirt field. At the bottom of the front cover were more symbols. One of the things Leo most hoped to find was among the various symbols spread along the bottom of the cover—the three letters *s, o,* and *d.*

"Amanda, do you remember seeing this word *sod* on the patches the teenagers were wearing?"

"Oh, Leo—yeah that's what they had on their arms! What else did you find in that book?"

"I haven't looked yet. I'm kind of scared, too, you know. It's called *Visions into the Fantastic.* I kind of don't want to know what those guys are up to if it's too dark—you know what I mean?"

CHAPTER EIGHT

Ghost Stories on the Corner

"What are you going to tell Blaine?"

Leo answered Amanda with a shrug of his shoulders. After a couple of minutes, he let out a huge sigh. "It's just all too weird, Amanda—it's just too weird. I think there is more to all this than a crazy dream of mine. Hey, you go to church on Sundays. Do you ever hear of stuff like this in the stories from the Bible?"

Leo had never admitted to Amanda how interested he was in the stories Mrs. Borland would tell in Sunday School when he visited.

Amanda shook her head as she answered. "No, nothing like this—but I don't know all of the stuff in the Bible. It's a pretty thick book."

"Well, maybe it's time for some digging in there, too."

Amanda and Leo finished up at the library and walked until they were a block away from their street. It took them over a half hour of slow walking back to Lakeside Drive. They normally would have made the walk in about ten or fifteen minutes, but their thoughts caused them to dawdle on their way home.

It was a sunny Saturday afternoon, with many families out in their yards. Lakeside Drive and the adjoining streets were never very busy with cars, so the streets were often filled with children of all ages playing, tossing or kicking balls, and riding bikes, scooters, and skateboards. The two friends could smell barbeques heating up in preparation for the evening's burnt offerings. Leo looked to his left and could see a smoky plume ascending behind the fence of the Fultons' house.

"The Fultons are having another barbeque. Are you going to be eating over there tonight?" Leo asked, because Amanda and her family often had dinner there.

"Not tonight. I heard they were going to eat early this Saturday, because they have to be at the airport at 7:00. They're going to Hawaii."

"Must be nice." Leo raised his eyebrows and slowly shook his head. He could only imagine what it must be like to get on a plane and go anywhere at all. He hoped that someday, he would be rich enough to be able to go on a trip on an airplane. The Fultons went on a trip about every other month—even during the school year.

The Fulton family didn't seem to fit into the neighborhood very well. They were nice enough people, but they had more money than any of the other families on the street. They would smile and wave, as nice neighbors do, but they didn't usually mix with the other families. The rumor on the street was that the dad was a golfer. This meant the family was often at some country club. None of the kids had ever seen this club, but they had heard and imagined that there were a lot of snobby rich folks there who probably didn't take too much interest in kids. Blaine and Leo joked that all the kids on Lakeside Drive would probably be looked at like Dennis the Menace by the friends of the Fultons at the country club.

Frank, Louis, and the other guys often cracked jokes. Even though the Fultons were nice and polite, most of the kids got the feeling they didn't really like kids—they just put up with children, like many adults did.

When Amanda and her family were invited to a barbeque, it was the only interaction the Fultons had with anyone else on the block. That was noticed by Leo and the other kids, because all the kids on the block had been in every other house on the street many times—but not the Fultons' home. The parents of the other families were so comfortable and familiar with most of the kids that often, neighborhood kids would just announce themselves and walk in without waiting for an invitation. The kids weren't being rude; the neighbors just knew each other well, and the kids were usually mutual friends with all of the other families.

That was another thing that stood out about the Fultons—they only had one kid. They were the only family on the block that didn't have at least two kids. There were grandmas and grandpas, cousins and nephews, and aunts and uncles all bunched together on a few adjoining blocks, but Leo didn't know of any other family that only had one kid. It seemed odd to him.

The Fultons had moved in about nine months ago. The father had a nice job in Chicago, and his company had transferred him to the West Coast to help the newer branch. Their son, Timothy, was Blaine's age. He was always inviting Amanda over for things. Just two months after moving into their home, the Fultons hired a company to install a pool and Jacuzzi. It was the only one on the block—or many blocks, for all Leo knew. Timothy invited Amanda over for a swim a few times—but never any of the other kids.

"You guys don't like Timothy, do you?" Amanda had guessed it but never said anything about it.

"You guys? What do you mean, you guys? Who are you talking about?"

"You and your brother and Frank—and, well, none of the kids around here seem to like him. Well, do you?"

"I don't know . . . we don't know him; he goes to some private school. He never plays outside. He just swims in his pool or goes to the country club. I'm sure he's nice, but we don't ever see him."

"What country club?"

"I don't know. I thought his family goes to some country club and hangs out with rich people, playing golf."

"It's people his dad works with, I think."

"How come he invites you to go swimming in his pool, and none of us ever get to go?"

"Oh, Leo, I don't know. Let's forget that. We need to decide what to tell your brother about what we found at the library."

Leo got the not-so-subtle hint that Amanda was done talking about Timothy. "They're probably at Frank and Louis's house. They probably finished their game a while ago."

Distracted by their thoughts and then the Fultons' barbeque, Leo and Amanda never noticed that the librarian's assistant had followed them home. She was never too close—almost out of sight at times—but close enough to see where they were going. She stood at the end of the block, in front of the Fultons' house, and watched as Leo and Amanda walked past Leo's house and into Frank and Louis's house. After seeing that they had gone into the house, she turned back in the direction she had come and quickly left.

Leo opened the door for Amanda and let her go in first. From behind her, Leo raised his hand and gave a silent greeting to the guys. They were sprawled on the couch with a bag of chips and some sodas in front of them. They looked relaxed and comfortable with their feet propped up on the coffee table. The grass and mud from their shoes had started to litter the small table. Some chips that didn't make it to their mouths were scattered on their shirts and pants.

"Oh! Look at this!" Louis taunted. "It's the bookworms, finally come home. Guess what you missed out on, little man?"

"You're not so big yourself, Louis," Leo offered back to his friend.

"Louis, leave Leo alone." Amanda was quick to defend Leo.

"Have you two been at the library all this time? They must be giving away money or something." Blaine was joking with his brother, but he was still upset that his team had lost. When he played with his brother, Blaine rarely lost. He had to take Frank and Louis's boasting all by himself.

"We lost, Leo. Thanks a lot. You spent time reading books, and I got jawed at all the way home from these guys."

"I'm sorry, Blaine," Leo responded, "but I had to find some answers if I could about those kids and what they might be up to."

"Well, did you find anything in those books?" Blaine asked.

"I think we did." Leo paused and gave some more thought to what he and Amanda had found. "I think those kids are called the Sons of Darkness."

"What?" Frank, Louis, and Blaine all stirred and sat up at that announcement.

"It's pretty wild stuff, guys," Leo continued. "Those teenagers weren't just playing with fire and singing campfire songs."

"No, I didn't think so. So what's up? What did you find, Leo?" Blaine was listening, curious.

"Well," Leo started, "Amanda and I looked at a lot of books, and I found one that had many symbols from some dark and ritualistic sects."

"Dark what? Did I hear you right?" Frank asked.

"There are many religious groups in the world, Frank, and they can be called *sects.* It's a funny name, I know—and it sounds like something else—but let's go on." Leo continued, hoping to get back on topic. "Okay, in the books, I saw a lot of weird symbols, but one that I saw a few times was the one those teenagers had on the patch on their right arm. The three letters are short for Sons of Darkness. They think they follow some dark angels or the Devil or something."

"Oh, gosh—so we got Devil kids hanging around in our town?" Louis shot back in disgust.

"Never mind my brother. Keep going, Leo," Frank said.

"That's what it looks like, Louis. I didn't find out anything about this Nephi they keep talking about, and I don't know if that is what they call the tall kid or not. I do know that there was a giant man or something in my dream."

"Whoa! Your dream?" Frank leaned forward, as though he was going to get up, but then leaned back, ran both hands through his hair, and laced his fingers together behind his head. "You didn't say anything about a dream. You dreamt this stuff, too?"

Amanda came to his rescue. "He wasn't going to tell you guys that. I guess it sort of slipped out—huh, Leo?"

Leo nodded, felling a little embarrassed.

Louis reached over to Leo, grabbed his forearm, and looked right into his eyes. "Quiet man, did you dream about those teenagers too?"

Leo met his stare and just nodded a few times for emphasis.

"Are you kidding me, man? This is crazier than a bunch of teenagers playing with fire in the night." He looked over at Blaine. "Blaine, you didn't tell me your brother was some, like, psychic or something."

"He's not a psychic, Louis," Blaine replied. "He just had a bad dream, and somehow he saw some things that were like his dream. That's all. Let's not get crazy here. Leo, tell you what—let's get home for now. I know you have more to tell us, but let's get back together after we've all had some dinner. Mom probably is out of bed by now—or maybe even gone—so let's go check in, and we can go over more of this later."

"It's going to be a great night for spooky ghost stories—I can tell." Frank was genuinely excited about hearing more of what Leo had to say.

"You guys get out of here. Get your chores done, or get some din-din before your mom heads out again. Amanda, you gotta come back, too. Will your parents let you come back?"

"Yeah, I think it will be fine—but we can't be too long. I've got church in the morning."

"That's cool." Frank said. "Let's say we meet back at 7:00 on the corner in front of the Fultons' house."

CHAPTER NINE

A Flash, a Fire, and a Fatal Mistake

The kids got to their chores and wolfed down their dinners. After warding off probing questions from their parents and efforts to get them to stay at home, they all managed to get out of the house in time to get to the corner by 7:00. Leo and Blaine never talked more about what Leo found at the library while they were at home. Blaine figured he would let Leo spill it all when the guys got back together later.

It was a warm night in late fall. The good weather was not unusual on the West Coast, but the days were getting shorter, so the sun had been set for almost two hours by the 7:00 meeting time. There was a very light breeze that sent the aroma of sweet anise through the neighborhood. Wild anise grew in the field, and the kids sometimes broke off pieces and chewed on the stalks. It tasted a little like black licorice but with a natural, weedy flavor.

The streetlights were on, but they weren't bright enough to outshine many of the brightest stars. The moon was past full and low on the horizon. It could be seen just above the line of sycamore trees past the empty field at the edge of the intersection of Lakeside Drive and Maple. It was a good night to be out, and a few people were, but none were on the street. Those who were out were resting on their front porches or in their backyards, enjoying the comfortable temperature.

Though all the kids had to rush, and some parents were curious about their activities, they managed to get out the door and down to the corner in front of the Fultons' by the agreed-upon time.

"Hey, guys," Amanda greeted everyone.

"Hi, Amanda." The guys, all on cue, responded in kind.

"Perfect night for a spooky story, Leo, right here under the streetlight." Frank encouraged Leo to spur him on.

"Yeah, and right across the street from the field where we all nearly died!" Louis added.

"Nobody almost died, but the moon is a little creepy tonight." Blaine said. "All we need is a black cat, and we'll be all set." Blaine noticed the moon from where they stood. Looking at the moon from his vantage point, he could barely see anything in the empty field. It just looked dark and ominous and added to the suspense as they prepared to hear what Leo had to say. Dark nights worked like that sometimes. Though the kids knew all that was in the field, sometimes the darkness made them think about what kinds of ghouls and goblins might be lurking close by.

"The field is giving me the creeps right now." Blaine turned his back to it, and the others followed his example.

"Okay, Leo, I didn't hear what you said earlier, so now I'm real curious about what you found at the library." Eric had been called, and he joined the group for the story.

"Are we going to make the Fultons wonder what we're doing out here in front of their house?" Eric asked.

"No, they won't, Eric," Amanda said. "They called our house to let my parents know that they had left for the airport and won't be back until the Tuesday after next."

"Just like the Fultons—little Timmy gets to go on vacation while we have to keep going to school." Frank said what many of them thought.

Amanda didn't like his comment and gave him a dirty look to let him know. Lightly slapping Frank's shoulder, she said, "Leave him alone, Frank. He's got a family who has money. So what? If you were in a family like that, someone would be making fun of you going on vacation too, so just shut up."

"Okay, little miss. Sorry, I didn't mean to talk about your boyfriend." Frank egged her on.

"Frank, cool it. Besides, Leo is Amanda's boyfriend, not little Timmy." Blaine tried to keep the peace but couldn't help from throwing a little jab at Leo at the same time.

Amanda leaned over, wrapped both arms around Leo, and squeezed tight. "Yes, dear, tell us a story, please." She batted her eyes to play up the part. This caused Leo to blush bright red and shake his head.

Eric came to Leo's rescue. "Okay, guys. I came to listen to Leo, not everyone else. Let's jump up on the Fultons' wall and sit, since they're not here. There's good light here, and it will make a great spot." Everyone looked at the three-foot stone wall and decided to hop on at once with an "Alley-oop!" from Louis.

"Hey!"

"What the . . ."

Frank was shoved completely over the wall mid-jump, and Blaine was shoved head-first into the stone. Eric received a sharp blow to the ribs that caused him to let out a howl as he leaned over in intense pain. Louis turned and tried to strike back but was shoved by two teenagers into the wall. His back struck the rough stone as his head slammed hard. Woozy and teary-eyed, he held his arms over his head to guard against any further blows. Leo and Amanda were both grabbed but not struck.

A small pack of about ten teenagers surrounded the kids. Some had sticks, but all had evil intent. Two others who had jumped over to where Frank landed pulled him up and shoved him against the wall. They held him there against the rough stone. Fresh blood oozed out of cuts on his face.

Anger and malice stirred in Frank's face as he tried to spy out his captors. Leo could see he was already plotting his escape and trying to find something to whack some kids with.

A quick glance at the group revealed to Leo some unfriendly but familiar faces. He saw Lug and the other two who had chased him and his friends through the field the previous night. He also saw the kid they called Craze. He had a far-off, spacey look in his eye that made Leo think he might be the most dangerous of them all.

"Okay, here's the deal, little kids!" Lug spoke sternly but didn't want to draw attention from any adults who might notice a crowd at the end of the block. "We don't want to hurt you much—maybe a little payback for the guy who wacked my knee. But the rest of you—we just want to do one thing."

"What's that one thing, Craze?"

"We're gonna scare them, right, Lug?"

"That's right, Craze. We're gonna scare 'em. You all did us a big favor by coming out here to the end of the street. We've been sitting over in the field, waiting and watching for you, and looky here—you come right down here for us. Well, here's what we're gonna do. Little lady, you gave us an idea. We heard you say the people who live here aren't home. Well, we're gonna pay them a little visit while they're gone. We're gonna break in that house so we can have a little privacy, so everyone over the fence—now!"

At Lug's command the teens helped shove, lift, or throw the kids over the wall. The two who had Frank shoved him to the ground. Frank immediately popped up and faced them, but as he did, several of the other teens circled around him. Frank glared back at all of them. He knew he was outmatched, so he held his ground. His chest rose and fell as he breathed heavily. Adrenaline pounded through his veins.

“You’re the kid who whacked me, aren’t you?” Lug leaned over the shoulder of one of the kids who circled around Frank. “We’re not messing around this time, kid, and you better not be swinging any sticks, or we might just break a few on your head this time. Now, let’s get to the backyard and get in that house.”

Leo knew this was not going to turn out well. In his dreams, he often imagined himself as a great warrior. This time, though, he knew he wasn’t dreaming. This was real. He could only hope that a friend would show up to help, because he was scared to go into the house with the teens. He thought about the dark building in his dream. *I have to watch for a way to escape. I can’t let Blaine or Amanda get hurt. What should we do? There’s too many of them. We can’t go in there with them.* Leo started to panic. He could see fear on the faces of all his friends. Instinctively, he grabbed Amanda’s hand. She said nothing, but he saw the panic in her eyes when she looked at him. Without words, she seemed to beg him to do something. He wanted to, but he felt helpless.

All the kids were really scared. They looked hopefully down the street, desperately hoping to catch the eye of at least one adult or someone who noticed what had happened. All the families knew the kids and would surely have come to their defense if they had seen what had happened. But they were on their own in the backyard and out of sight from any potential help.

“Craze, take your shirt off!” Lug commanded.

“What for?” Craze protested.

“I said, take it off. You want the Nephi to hear of your rebellion?”

Leo’s ears perked up at the mention of the Nephi. *I hope he’s not going to show up, too.* He noticed the immediate obedience from Craze at the mention of the Nephi. Craze took his shirt off, and Lug grabbed a stick from one of the others. He wrapped the shirt around one end and approached the small bathroom window.

"Jones, Barnes, set up a watch at the corners of the house. I'm going to break this window." Lug barked the orders, and the two boys hurried over to peek around the sides of the house as Lug used the padded stick to break the window. The stick and Craze's shirt fell inside the house.

"Man, my shirt!" Craze objected.

"Shut up about your shirt, Craze!" Lug turned and got in his face. "Maybe we should use some of that glass to finish your back."

Craze just dipped his head and mumbled something. Leo looked at Craze's back and cringed at what he saw. His back was laced up and down with scores of jagged edged lines that looked to be the remnants of some wicked cuts. A couple of them looked red and tender. *I wonder if all these kids have backs like that. Is that what the sons of darkness do to one another?* Leo wondered.

Lug yelled at Craze again. "Now crawl in there, and get your shirt. While you're in there, go around and get the door open for us. Can you do that?"

"Yes, I can do that." Craze obeyed, but Leo could sense the venom in his voice as he responded to Lug.

"Don't make me, Craze . . ." Lug threatened. He didn't finish the sentence.

Leo and his friends were afraid of the horrors Lug might have in mind for them once they all got inside. They tried to keep a low profile and hoped that Craze would take the heat that was intended for them.

Quickly after Craze shimmied through the window, he made his way through the dark house and opened the back sliding glass door.

"Now, everyone inside, and *nobody* better turn on any lights, because that would be stupid—and I don't like stupid people!" Lug was in charge of this group of teens. He spoke to them as though they were a bunch of half-wit children.

He's a dumb half-wit himself, most likely, Leo thought, wishing he could shout it out to everyone.

They all pushed inside. Several of the teens immediately plopped themselves down on the large, L-shaped sofa in the living room. Its big pillows and a white fluffy comforter were grabbed at and wrestled over. The strongest and most aggressive kids quickly won the battle for those. Two big reclining chairs were claimed. The fight for those sent a couple of the teens tumbling to the ground.

Lug stood in the middle and looked menacingly around at his band of minions. "You guys all comfortable now?" Some nodded; others could tell he didn't want a response. The look he gave them all said it was time to shut up and listen.

Leo and Amanda were still in the grasp of the two who had grabbed them. Their arms were held uncomfortably behind they backs. They winced whenever their captors tried to nudge them forward from the back of the pack. With all the others filling up the couch, chairs, and living room floor, the kids who held Leo and Amanda brought them just inside the house, near the edge of the sliding glass door. Frank, Louis, Blaine, and Eric were shoved down to the floor at the feet of Lug. The four hung their heads. They peeked up at times to steal glances at their surroundings, hoping to gauge who might be paying less attention. Their situation looked bad, but they hadn't given up on breaking away. They thought there might be a chance for escape if the teens got too wrapped up in their new, comfortable surroundings.

Lug grabbed their attention. "Okay, let's get this little meeting started." He slipped off his leather jacket and tossed it to the kid who flanked him on his right. He wore the same tight-fitting, long-sleeved black shirt that Leo had become accustomed to seeing. The familiar *sod* lettering appeared on his right sleeve.

Sons of Darkness. In his time in the library, Leo had concluded the lettering referred to the Sons of Darkness. *Offspring from hell is more like it.* Leo smoldered in anger at the hatred and evil he sensed coming from Lug. He had expected to see the lettering on the shirt—but not the knife he suddenly noticed.

The knife rested on Lug's left hip. Braided leather strands dangled from its leather scabbard. A small silver skull swung from the end of one of the leather strips. Lug reached across his hip with his right hand and slowly pulled the blade from its sheath.

Nobody spoke. Everyone was riveted on the blade as Lug admired it. He slid his left thumb across its polished edge.

"It's sharp. Anyone want to find out how sharp?"

Nobody dared to move or speak a word. Lug slowly slid his thumb up the blade toward the tip. As he did, a slight crimson flow trickled from his thumb onto the blade. He watched it—as did everyone else—until it began to drip onto the clean, carpeted floor. The drops of blood splattered on the soft carpet in front of Blaine.

"Craze, get over here!"

Craze, who had been in the kitchen, looking over the counter, hustled to stand next to Lug.

"Sit down," Lug commanded as he pointed at a spot just to the left of Blaine and in front of Frank.

Craze looked nervous but didn't question Lug. He hadn't finished fishing the glass shards out of his shirt, so he was still bare-chested. The scar tracks on his back were close enough for Blaine and Frank to get a better look than they hoped for. Lug looked at the four young boys who sat close enough to see the painful-looking back of Craze. A devious grin eased onto Lug's face. He chuckled at the nervous looks on the faces of the boys and Craze.

"Okay, everyone." Lug spoke calmly and slowly. "We had some visitors to our meeting last night—some unwelcome visitors. We don't like unwelcome visitors, do we, Craze?"

"No, sir, we don't," Craze quickly replied, averting his eyes.

"We might consider forgiveness for those who are interested in joining with us. Each one of you is young and useful, though one of you is a girl." Lug paused and looked behind him to direct a wicked eye toward Amanda. "Even girls have purpose sometimes—right, Craze?"

"Yes, sir," said Craze.

Amanda, who was still held firmly back by the sliding glass door, met his glare but immediately looked away. She shivered in fear and tried to pull her arm away from the teen who held her tight. This only tightened the grip the young man had on her. She began to feel desperate, as she and her friends were in an awful position.

"As you can see by the little scratches on the back of our friend Craze here, the initiation to our group can sometimes be a little painful. Craze is now one of our most loyal members, and he understands the need to follow orders. Isn't that right, Craze?"

"Yes, sir." Craze was careful to meet Lug's stare.

This guy has a wicked hold on these poor guys. They all must be stupid or scared to stay in this group. Leo started to feel pity for Craze and the other kids. He could tell they were all getting uncomfortable and nervous.

"Now for you little ones—we will forgive your intrusion at our meeting if your curiosity was your way of letting us know you want to join with us. Who would like to go first and offer the blood of approval to the cup of suffering? Craze, get up now, and go into these nice people's kitchen and find me a cup or a glass of some kind."

Craze immediately got up and ran to find his way back to the kitchen.

"Only a small offering of your blood is required to show your devotion to the Nephi's guidance. Shall it be ladies first?" He glanced back at Amanda, who was trembling. Her heart raced, and her throat tightened as she struggled to breathe.

"What is it you want from us?" Leo saw the fear in Amanda and immediately came to her rescue. He hoped to take Lug's attention off her.

"You, yes—um, I believe your name is Leo. Is that right?"

"Yes, sir." Leo tried to be brave, but he didn't feel brave, as his legs started to tremble.

"You are the one the Nephi is interested in. He speaks of you, though I don't see why. Somebody tells me you have been looking for information about the Nephi at the library. Is this true, Leo?"

Leo's legs shook, and sweat droplets ran down his back and the side of his face. His breath quickened. *The librarian's assistant—that must be who is helping him,* Leo thought. *That's why she was so interested in helping us.* Leo's mind raced through the things he had seen in his dreams and the real-life apparitions that were face-to-face with him. *How is this happening to me? How did I dream about these guys taking Blaine, and now they have taken us all? How can we ever get out of this?* He started to feel overwhelming dread. He looked around in his terror, hoping to see something less fearsome to give him a glimmer of hope of getting himself and his friends out.

"Well, boy, do you want to know about the Nephi or not? I have been told to bring you to him when I found you, and now I have found you," Lug mocked Leo. He could see Leo's fear.

Leo's legs were visibly shaking, and he struggled to keep himself from collapsing under the stare of Lug. He wanted to start ripping and twisting at the arm of the kid who held him and pummel him with his fists. If he did, he was sure other fists or sticks would rain down on him.

He had to escape—but his brother was in the middle of this frightening hoard of thugs.

Leo nervously looked back and forth, ignoring Lug and all the other sets of eyes that were now trained on him. He glanced to his left and caught a glimpse of a spectacularly bright light just outside. In the flash of its brilliance, he dared to hope it might be a flashlight of a neighbor or even the police. The light quickly grew in intensity and then expanded to the full size of the sliding glass door. Both bay windows and the slider suddenly shook violently, and the ground moved under Leo's feet.

"Whoa! Is that an earth . . ." someone started to speak, and then . . .

Kaboom!

Whoever had spoken was suddenly stopped in mid-sentence by a tremendous blast from the kitchen. Screams and yells rang out from everywhere. The couch had been jolted forward, and the kids on it were sprawled out on the floor. The explosion had hurled Craze over the counter and onto Lug, bringing them both down in a pile. They both moaned in pain. Craze's back was flayed open, and blood spilled from fresh wounds onto Lug and the floor.

Their chance had come. "Party's over, guys! Let's go, Louis!" Frank shouted as he grabbed his brother's shoulder and lifted him to his feet. Blaine and Eric, sprawled next to the groaning Lug and Craze, quickly got up and turned to find the door. The two boys who had held Leo and Amanda tight released their grip and were wobbling on their feet with stunned gazes on their faces.

The slider wasn't locked, so Leo threw it open, grabbed Amanda's hand, and pulled her with him through the opening. He turned left from where they had come in and led her to the stone fence in a sprint. "Can you jump?" he yelled.

"Yes!" She tightened her grip on his hand, and they both leaped onto the top of the stone wall and to the waiting sidewalk in one smooth motion. They sprinted out to the center of the street before turning to see who followed. They were relieved to see Eric, on the street side of the wall, helping Blaine, Frank, and Louis climb over. The three got to the sidewalk and raced to join Leo and Amanda.

"Wahoo!" Frank let out a primal scream.

They all glanced back to see if anyone followed. Seeing no one, they turned and sprinted up the street.

"What was that?" Blaine screamed as they ran. He, like the rest of them, couldn't believe the sudden turn and opportunity for escape that came at a moment of hopelessness and fear.

CHAPTER TEN

The Story Is Left Untold

As Leo, Blaine, and their friends ran up the street, they were met by a curious crowd of neighbors who were pouring out of their homes. The explosion had rocked much of the neighborhood. Recognizing the boys and Amanda coming from the direction of the blast, many ran to meet them. The blast was deafening to the kids, but they didn't expect the effect it would have on the whole block. Curious onlookers had come rushing out from every home to see the cause of what sounded like a huge explosion.

The kids were still in a bit of shock and clawed their way through and past the people plying them for answers to what had happened.

"Dad!" Louis saw both his parents and his two younger sisters out in their front yard.

"Louis, Frankie—did you boys see what happened?" Their father was happy and relieved to see his sons.

"We sure did, Dad; we sure did! Tell 'em, Frankie!" Louis called his older brother by the pet name his father always called him. Frank didn't like it, but it was an affectionate name his father had for him. Hearing it around his friends usually made him uncomfortable, but it didn't bother him that night. He was relieved to be running up to his dad and happy to be called Frankie by his loving father. He didn't mind that his younger brother called him Frankie.

The group of friends gathered onto Frank's front yard to listen as Frank started to tell his father what happened. Curious neighbors gathered nearby on the sidewalk.

A huge cracking and splitting of wood drew everyone's attention back to the Fultons' home. A portion of the roof had given way to the heat of the fire that was threatening to engulf the whole house. Flames could be seen inside the windows of the home. From out of the newly formed cavity in the roof, a large, billowing cloud of black smoke filled the sky.

Frank, who had started to tell his story stood in disbelief, watched with all the others as the flames licked at the sides of the home, trying desperately to consume it all before it could be rescued.

Then Blaine started laughing out loud. Leo looked over at him. Initially, Leo was surprised by his brother's reaction, but the relief suddenly hit him, too. A huge smile broke across his face as he exclaimed, "That was so close, you guys! Are we even alive?" Leo dropped to his knees and started laughing out loud along with his brother. The grass was damp, but he didn't mind. Eric let out a big sigh, fell backwards onto the grass, and started to laugh, too.

Amanda had a different reaction. She walked over to Leo, sat down on the damp grass in front of him, and rested her two hands on his knees. She looked at him, and a flood of tears burst out. Her shoulders heaved as her emotions spilled out. She brought a hand up to hide her face as the anguish and relief overwhelmed her.

Frank's mom, Mrs. Hernandez, rushed to Amanda's side. "Oh, sweetie, what happened?" She hugged Amanda and rocked her gently, caressing her hair. Mrs. Hernandez looked up at her oldest son. "Frankie, were you kids involved in this? Is there something you have done wrong?

"No, Mom," Frank answered with an incredulous stare.

"Mom, this is the wildest thing in the world that just happened. Tell her, Frank. tell her." Louis was excited and wanted his brother to get to the story that had been stalled by the crashing roof of the Fultons' home. The growing crowd of familiar faces on the sidewalk listened in as they stared in awe at the fire that raged on the corner. An alarm was heard in the distance.

"Dad, we got kidnapped in that house!" Frank blurted out. His mother gasped at what her son said, as did the others on the sidewalk.

His father was not so sure and asked for more information. "Frankie, what do you mean you got kidnapped? You were just at the house for dinner. Where did you kids go? I thought I told you to stay on the street!"

"Dad, no—let me tell you what happened." Frank was flustered at his mom's reaction and his dad's questions. As Amanda continued to sob, he glanced around at the growing and curious crowd and started his story again. "Well, we all just went down to the corner and were standing under the streetlight there. Isn't that right, Blaine?" Frank looked to Blaine to back him up.

"That's right, Mister Hernandez; we were just on the corner—right there," Blaine said, corroborating his friend's story.

"So what do you mean you got kidnapped, Frankie?"

"Okay, Dad. See, we were all talking down under the streetlight, and all of a sudden, a bunch of teenagers came and jumped us and told us to jump over the Fultons' wall and break into the house."

"They told you to break into the house? Who, Frankie? Who? I don't see anybody else; I just see you six kids, and this poor little girl is all upset. Did you break into that house, Frankie?"

"*No,* Dad!" Both Frank and Louis were empathic in their response.

Louis turned to Leo. "Leo, can you tell my dad what happened? Dad, listen to Leo. You know he never messes around. He wouldn't lie to you. Tell him what happened, Leo."

The sidewalk crowd pressed in closer to get at the story. Whispers and comments were exchanged as the boys tried to muster up the best way to tell Mr. Hernandez what happened. Amanda had calmed down enough to raise her head and look at Mrs. Hernandez, who still held her tight. "They're telling the truth, Mrs. Hernandez."

With her words, Amanda started sobbing again and leaned into Mrs. Hernandez's shoulder. Mrs. Hernandez held her and rocked some more. She turned to her husband. "Dear," she told her husband, "something terrible has happened. Listen to the boys. This little sweetie says they are telling the truth."

"Mr. Hernandez," Leo started, "it happened really fast, but we were kidnapped, like Frank said. It was a bunch of teenagers. We didn't know them. They saw us on the corner. They just came up fast without us seeing them and made us go into the Fultons' backyard. The Fultons aren't home right now, so one of the teenagers broke a window and made us all go inside. They hit Frank pretty hard, slammed some of us into the wall, and the leader had a big knife he was threatening us with."

"Oh, Frankie, dearie, are you alright?" Mrs. Hernandez became more troubled when she heard about her son being hit.

A muttering and stirring in the crowd began. A once-distant siren rounded a corner a block away, and the fire truck could be heard coming down the street. People in the crowd began to turn from Frank's story and hustle down the street to get a better look at the firemen. The curious onlookers wanted to see if they could get another side of the story from what the fire department found on the inside of the house.

As the attention started to move away from Leo and his friends, Mr. Hernandez suggested they take everyone inside to get them a drink and let them all calm down before they tried to find out more of the story.

When everyone was inside the Hernandez home, Mr. Hernandez called the police to report what was going on down the street and what his son had told him about being kidnapped by an unknown group of teenagers. When he got off the phone with the police, he dialed Eric and Amanda's parents. There was no answer at either house. He figured their parents were out with everyone else, seeing what the turmoil was. "Blaine, is your mother home?" he asked.

"No, Mr. Hernandez," Blaine answered. "She was gone earlier today. She said she wouldn't be back until late."

"Well, then you and your brother can stay here as long as you want. Eric, Amanda, we should go outside to see if we can find your parents. They may be worried and looking for you."

"I'll just go home, sir," Eric offered. "I have a key and can let myself in. But if you don't mind, sir, I think I want to stay a little longer and see what the fire department finds."

"Okay. That's fine, Eric," Mr. Hernandez replied. "Amanda, are you feeling better? Do you mind if we go outside now and try to find your parents?"

Amanda nodded. "Yes, that's fine. I'm okay now. It was just so very scary. If that explosion didn't happen, they were going to hurt us. I can't believe we got out of there so quickly." Her eyes glazed over with tears again, but she was able to compose herself. "I'm fine—really. I still can't believe what just happened."

Leo felt horrible as he watched Amanda cry, emotionally exhausted from the ordeal. He was shaken up by it, too, and he knew there would be a lot of questions to follow when the police and fire department started asking about what happened.

What did happen? What was that bright light outside the house before the explosion? Did anyone else see that? What caused the explosion? Was it Craze messing with the stove? He did like to play with fire. Leo pondered the unanswered questions. *The firemen will find out what happened.*

CHAPTER ELEVEN

Christmas Tears

Leo and Blaine couldn't believe it was finally Saturday. It was 8:00 in the morning, and they sat on their front lawn, waiting. They slouched on their hastily packed duffle bags filled with clothes, shoes, and other things the boys thought they would need for the next two weeks. The events of the past month were far from their minds that morning.

The police had asked many questions of all the kids. The questioning began outside the Fultons' house and spread to each of their individual homes. They then made a couple trips to the police department. Leo was especially nervous being there. He asked Blaine about it later, and Blaine said he was nervous at the police station, too. Leo felt that at times, the police were trying to find something he and his brother had done wrong. Sometimes it felt that way for kids. It seemed to Leo that adults often thought kids were lying, and it was their job to figure out what kids lied about. The whole story was a bit strange, though. Leo could understand why people expected there to be more to it.

Leo never said anything about his dreams or the bright light he saw outside the house just before the explosion. He just stuck to the part about the teenagers taking them into the house and threatening them.

The kids were stunned to find out that both Craze and Lug had died. Craze was too close to the explosion and suffered severe burns and other internal injuries as he was thrown from the point of the blast. He died after a week in the hospital. Lug had died from a knife wound.

When the police entered the home after the fire was put out, they found Lug dead at the scene. The handle of a large knife was sticking out of his chest when they rolled him over.

Leo thought the death of Lug was what troubled the police the most. They had hoped to find out more information about how it happened. The kids could only guess. They told the police all they knew. The police did what they had to do so often in these cases; they put the pieces together as best they could.

The papers said Lug's real name was Anthony Peterson. Quotes from his parents said he was a good kid who planned to go to college and become a dentist.

A dentist—I bet he would have loved to pull teeth. Leo thought it curious at the time as he read the story in the newspaper. He thought Lug's parents probably had no idea what their son was doing with that mysterious group of teenagers.

The police found unknown prints in the home of the Fultons and determined these must have been from the other teenagers involved. Nobody else was found or connected to the crime. Leo didn't think the police were very interested in pursuing the crime any further. The death of Lug and Craze should have been warning enough for the unknown teenagers to stay away from such activities in the future.

The fire department had determined the explosion to be the result of an accidental fire caused by a faulty gas line. There wasn't enough evidence to determine what caused the spark or ignition that caused the gas to explode.

Leo had seen the bright light, and felt the shaking before the explosion, so he knew there was more to the story than a faulty gas line. He kept that to himself though. He and Amanda could work on solving that later.

Leo and Blaine sat on their lawn on the first Saturday morning of Christmas vacation, eagerly waiting. They hadn't seen their father since summer vacation, when they were able to stay with him a whole month.

"Dad's coming, Leo!" Blaine let out a quiet but excited scream. He didn't want their mother to hear. She knew her ex was coming to pick up the boys, but she would be mad if the boys showed their excitement in front of her, so they usually tried to keep it to themselves.

"I know, Blaine. I am so happy he is finally almost here." When their dad's Cadillac finally turned the corner, they couldn't contain their excitement.

"Dad!" Leo jumped up first and waved both his hands to get his father's attention.

"He sees us, Leo. He won't pass us by." Blaine was just as excited, but being a year older, he felt the need to look more mature and controlled.

Their father pulled the dark blue Cadillac up to the curb, and the boys could see the huge grin on his face. Both boys started to tear up a bit at the sight of their beloved father. They left their duffle bags and ran out to the driver's side of the car to greet their father.

"Hi, boys! Get your bags; don't you think you might need them?"

Blaine and Leo ignored his words and leaped on him. Each hugged whatever part of him they could get a hold of. Their father gladly hugged them back. Tears streamed down the cheeks of both of the boys, which they tried to hide by burying their faces in their father's chest. He hugged them some more and caressed their heads, giving them time to regain their composure.

"Well, men, we have a long drive ahead of us. I'll open the trunk while you grab your bags." With his face safely hidden behind the trunk lid, their father was able to wipe the tears that had formed in the corner of his eyes. These greetings and departures were always very emotional for the boys and their father. The heartbreak of a broken family was easy to see on such days.

The trip up the freeway was over two hours, but it felt like a chauffeur-driven ride in a limousine for the boys. They weren't used to such a fancy car, and the stop at the fast food burger place with an order of large fries and a chocolate shake was as good as the boys could ever hope for.

They could not have been happier. Blaine did most of the talking, as was usually the case. He filled in their dad on all the things that were going on. Their dad just nodded, laughed, or winked at both sons as Blaine told the stories of their life on Lakeside Drive over the past few months.

The boy's father was an investment broker who had never remarried. He enjoyed his work and the pleasures and benefits it brought, but he took his greatest pleasure in having time with his boys. They always returned home with more gifts and new clothing than they could even carry.

The first few days in their father's home were filled with unmatched bliss. Leo and Blaine took trips to the beach, went to the park, and tossed footballs and baseballs in their dad's front yard. The boys couldn't stop smiling most of the time. They had lots of fun, but Wednesday couldn't come soon enough. This was the day the boys had most looked forward to.

"Can you boys hang on to these?" their father asked as he handed each of them a small packet.

"What are they, Dad?" Blaine asked.

"These are the ticket books. There are A tickets and B tickets, and more in there, but the best tickets are the E tickets." The boys' dad opened the packet he held and showed them each of the tickets.

"What's the E ticket for, Dad?"

"Let me show you, Blaine." He gathered both boys close. "At the bottom of the ticket, you can read what rides you can go on with each ticket."

"How do we get on the Matterhorn?" Blaine asked.

"That's the E ticket. You boys want to go on that first?"

"Yes!" Blaine and Leo both clutched their ticket books and hopped excitedly as they glanced at the lines of people slowly shuffling toward the front gates that would free them all to explore the "happiest place on earth." Other people in the line smiled knowingly at the excitement on the faces of Blaine and Leo.

Long lines, fast rides, costumed characters, and monorails dazzled the brothers and captivated their attention all morning and into the night. They stopped for food at the Mexican diner just past the shooting gallery in Frontierland. The boys were starving and tired and enjoyed the chance to rest and take pleasure in watching the masses of people coming and going. The lights were spectacular, and the splendor of the park was amazing. The boys lifted their feet as a park attendant came by, sweeping up trash into his dust pan with the long handle.

"That's so cool that he can pick all that up and never have to bend over for it," Leo said.

"I know. We need one of those for at home," Blaine said.

"That would be great, Blaine," Leo answered.

"This place is so much fun!" exclaimed Blaine. "Thanks, Dad!"

"You're welcome, Blaine. I'm having as much fun as you are, boys. I have always enjoyed this place."

"Me too, Dad," said Leo. "Thanks for taking us. Can we go on Pirates again? I think that's my favorite ride."

"Oh, is it? What happened to the Matterhorn?" Leo's dad shot back.

"That's great, too, but I like Pirates, 'cause it's longer, and it looks so real down there. Dead men don't tell no tales, Dad."

The boys' father laughed out loud at Leo's mimicking of the voice over the loudspeaker in the Pirates ride.

"Yes, Leo, we can go on Pirates again. It's not too far from here, so when we finish eating, we can go find the line. It's just a little ways over there." He pointed in the direction of the big steamboat that floated by on the small, man-made lake. It glided past Tom Sawyer's Island, where lots of kids could be seen running through and over the dirt trails, looking for Indians and trappers as they imagined themselves in a Mark Twain story.

Leo eagerly finished scooping up the remaining beans and rice on his plate. His cheese enchilada was long since gone, and he was tempted to use his finger to wipe up what remained on his plate.

Twilight was upon the park. Thousands of lights twinkled on the buildings and plants all around them. The smell of Mexican food was strong, but it didn't completely drown out the aroma of popcorn, cotton candy, and even the gunpowder from the shooting gallery around the corner.

Leo and Blaine couldn't keep themselves from constantly looking all around and sizing up the sights and smells of the day. It was the greatest day they'd had in a long time. Often during the day, they could be seen holding their father's hand while standing in line or running to the next "land" that the park offered for them to explore.

"How much longer before we have to leave, Dad?" Leo asked.

"We can stay till 12:00, son."

"Really? That's so cool!" Leo had never stayed up until 12:00 before.

"Twelve o'clock? Nice—really, Dad, are we going to stay that long?" Blaine asked, excited.

"Yes, Blaine, we can stay till 12:00. Let's get going to Pirates of the Caribbean. Pick up your trays, boys, and let's set them over there on the counter."

The boys followed their dad's lead as he set his tray and dinner plate where a stack of used dishes was collecting.

"Whoa! Look at all those, Leo," Blaine blurted.

"I wouldn't want to do all those dishes." Leo agreed.

"I know. I guess our sink full of dishes at home isn't so bad after all."

The boys followed their father's leading and pushed into the press of people that filtered out of the dining area and into the mass of humanity on the street. With big smiles on their faces, they walked and occasionally skipped with excitement as they made their way through the crowd of people. They felt small, as almost everyone towered above them. They kept their eyes on their father, but he never went too fast and always made sure they were right at his side.

They approached the walkway to get in line for Pirates when Blaine stopped abruptly and gave Leo a swift backhand to his left arm.

"Hey, what was that for?" Leo's smile turned to a puzzled frown.

"Look!" Blaine pointed to their right in the mass of people that flowed past.

"What am I supposed to be looking at?" Leo protested.

"Boys, we need to keep moving. What are you stopping for?" their father asked.

"Okay, Dad. We were just looking at everything," Blaine responded. The boys caught up to their dad and were soon at the back of the line for the Pirates ride.

"Leo!" Blaine pulled on his brother's arm to draw him close as he spoke in his ear.

"What is wrong with you, Blaine?" Leo protested again. Blaine pointed again. "Okay, what is it you want me to look at?"

"See that stand there where they're selling the lollipops?" Blaine asked.

"Yes, is that what you . . ." Leo stopped in mid-sentence.

"Now do you see them?"

"Yes, yes, I see them. Do you think they are from the same group?"

"They're different, Leo. Those are not the same kids." Blaine sounded concerned—and he looked it.

"I know, but that patch is the same; the clothes are the same. They must somehow be connected to those other kids."

"I'm pretty sure you're right, Leo. What kind of a group is this? Is it some gang or something that's in different cities?"

Just to the right of the candy cart where the vendor sold lollipops and other sweets was a group of about fifteen teenagers. Most were boys, but about four or five girls mixed in. They stood out from the surrounding crowd because of their black clothes and the now-familiar patch on the right sleeves with the letters that spelled *sod.* Leo had determined the letters probably meant Sons of Darkness, but he wasn't sure.

"I thought we were getting away from them." Leo stared at the group of teens. He was glad he didn't see an unusually tall one in their midst. He had started to wonder if the tall one was the Nephi that Lug had talked about. The Nephi had asked about him and wanted to meet him. That's what Lug had said; Leo hoped it wasn't true.

"Blaine, Leo, you need to move up!" The boys' father had followed the slow-moving line and was inside the New Orleans-style gate that signaled the start of the fantasy.

"Sorry, Dad. We're coming," Blaine said as he and Leo ran to catch up to their father.

"Keep moving, boys; these lines don't wait. I didn't even notice you weren't following."

"We're sorry, Dad. We were just noticing things. There is so much to see here," Blaine fibbed. He didn't want to tell his dad what he was pointing out to Leo.

Now there was more to the mystery. There were more teens in a different city many miles away from where Leo lived. What was this group all about? It troubled Leo the rest of the night.

CHAPTER TWELVE

Lion Horses and the Nephi

Leo hesitated when he saw the giant oak tree. *I shouldn't be here. What if I fail?* He glanced back along the trail he had followed, drew in a deep breath, and raised the longbow to level in front of him. He drew an arrow from his scabbard and placed it at the ready in his bow. Silence would be to his advantage.

He eased his way toward the giant oak. His feet never made a sound. His deerskin shoes took him silently over the rocks, gravel, and leaves. Only an experienced tracker would have ever known he had been this way.

He set his sight on the large granite rock up to the left and made his way toward it. One of the large branches of the oak tree had grown up along the granite boulder and long ago bent its way up the side until it breached the top of the huge stone and continued its way unhindered by the stone as it stretched high into the sky. Leo stepped into the piles of acorns, leaves, and sticks the winds had gathered at the base of the large boulder. Still, his feet never made a sound.

The low shrubs growing between the stone and the oak were enough to hide him as he peered into the secret meeting of the dark angels. Before he saw them, he could smell their rank odor. It was sulfurous for sure, but it also reminded him of ammonia. Taking in too much at once would burn his nostrils and cause him to recoil from the harshness of their stench.

Now he could see them. From where Leo stood, they looked like quarter horses. Strong hindquarters housed muscles that bulged and rippled the skin on their back haunches. The muscles and tendons tightened as the dark angels leaped and lunged in their circular dance around the Nephi.

Up close, Leo could also see the distinctive feature of the animals—if they could be called animals. Their heads were like those of female lions. On these heads were cat-like features—the characteristic eyes of a cat, yellowed with distinctive feline pupils. They had prominent teeth with the extended canine fangs and jaw teeth of the female version of the king of the jungle. They appeared to be the result of some bizarre and cruel experiment.

The Nephi sat at the center of the circle as the lion horses performed what looked to be a prance of worship around the Nephi. Their heads all turned to the center of the circle as they seemed to mimic the prance of show horses on display. They never turned their gaze from the Nephi in the center of their parade.

The Nephi was seated, but his great height was still obvious. He held an open book in his hand. It had a black cover, and the pages were darker still. Leo couldn't see the front of the cover or anything on the pages. The Nephi's large hands held the book in his lap as he sat in the circle of lion horses.

Though he was sitting, his head was as tall as the horses who circled him. His face and body were that of a man, but he appeared to be eerily too perfect. He looked chiseled in stone like a perfect work of art Michelangelo would have carved in marble—only this marble moved. His eyes were on fire. He turned his head ever so gracefully to acknowledge those who circled him. As he did, Leo caught glimpses of the pupils in his eyes. Instead of the usual colored iris of the human eye that allowed light to pass to the retinue, the eyes of the Nephi had pupils of fire. It was unsettling to see little flames of fire in the eyes of that face—a face that looked to be that of a well-chiseled man. The feet of the Nephi were those of a goat—just his hind legs. His hands and arms were those of a normal man. They looked to be thick and strong.

Leo couldn't comprehend what evil intentions had brought about such seemingly wicked creations, nor did he really care. He was there to put an arrow through the heart of the giant Nephi and to put an end to its evil intentions—whatever they may be. He had a clear shot from where he hid behind the bushes. His skills at silence had gotten him this close, but once he let his arrow fly, his presence would be known. He didn't imagine he could outrun any of the lion horses. His plan was to quickly and silently disappear into the darkness and hope they would pass him in their pursuit.

He raised his bow, pulled back the string, and rested his left thumb on his cheek. He held his hand steady there. He could have held that position for many minutes without any effort. His strength had grown through years of training. He watched the pace of the lion horses to anticipate the best time to shoot lest one of them take the arrow instead of the Nephi. He counted quietly to himself to keep pace with their prance around the Nephi. "Almost . . . one, two, three . . ."

Thuuwump! Leo was shocked to see that a round granite stone about the size of his head had suddenly landed about six inches in front of him. The stone had been hurled at him from somewhere. He didn't know where it had come from, but when he looked back at the circle of lion horses, all motion had stopped, and they all were looking right over in his direction. The fiery eyes of the Nephi weren't fooled by the cover of the bushes and were looking right at Leo.

But Leo was more shocked to see an apparition hovering over the heads of the dark angels. The Shade appeared to take the shape of a lizard or wingless dragon-like creature. It appeared ghostlike as it hovered over the circle of lion horses. It seemed to shimmer and fade in and out of sight, but it was most definitely there, floating over the Nephi and his lion horses.

Out of the shimmering apparition, Leo could see another stone appear and start whistling toward him. Leo dove quickly to his left to hide behind the large granite boulder. The rock hurled by the apparition Thumped hard on the ground where he had just been.

Leo knew he needed to run but was afraid he wouldn't escape. He stole another quick glance at the vision. As he looked for the dragon creature, the dark night sky suddenly exploded in light. Laser-like rays of light streamed from something or someone that filled the sky behind the dragon that had hurled the stones at him. The lion horses and the Nephi were terror-stuck, and with lightning quickness, all of them launched into scattered sprints to escape this being of light.

The night sky was suddenly filled with the brightness of day. Little wisps of smoke rose from several spots on the ground where the rays of light had stuck the ground. There was no trace of any of the lion horses, and the Nephi had run far away.

Leo looked up at the terrible and awesome sight of the being in the sky. It appeared to be shrouded in an amber or golden lighted cloud. It was beautiful. Leo felt no fear of it at all. There was no sense of danger or any reason for Leo to run from it. He couldn't make out the form of the creature or its shape. It seemed human-like but too large, and at the edges was a glowing golden cloud. Rays of light streamed from it and spread in all directions of the night. Leo stared up at it in awe.

"Leo! Wake up, Leo; it's just a dream. You're all right son."

"Huh? Dad? Oh, I'm sorry; was I dreaming?"

"Yes, you were, son, and it was scaring me when I heard you. I heard two very loud thumps, and I came running in here to see what it was. Where is Blaine at?"

"Blaine—he's not here?" Leo shot up in his bed and looked over at the bed where his brother had been when they went to sleep last night.

"No, he's not here. Oh, Blaine, is that you?" The boys' father turned as he heard and then saw Blaine coming into the bedroom.

"Yeah, it's me. What's going on?" Blaine asked.

"It's your brother. He was having a pretty bad dream."

"Yeah, he started up a while ago, and I decided to try sleeping on the couch. He gets going pretty good sometimes."

"Leo, do you have bad dreams a lot?" their father asked.

"Not a lot—but yeah, I do have bad dreams sometimes. It's not a big deal; I just dream about regular things. But I guess if I'm battling dragons and stuff, then I just move around in my sleep a little. I'm sorry to wake you up, Dad."

"So now it's dragons, is it, Leo?" Blaine lifted his left eyebrow and shook his head.

"Leo, you don't need to apologize," his father said encouragingly. "I was just startled. What were the two loud thumps I heard?"

Leo thought about the two stones he saw hurled at him in his dream and realized that the loud thumping noise was real. "I really don't know. I was out until you just woke me."

"That's the way it is, Dad. I've been through it before. He's an active dreamer," Blaine added.

"An active dreamer, huh? Well, let's say we all get active. We only have two more days before I need to take you home to your mother."

"Uhgh! Dad, do you have to?" Blaine didn't want to hear that he and his brother's vacation was almost over. But more than the vacation, Leo and Blaine never enjoyed having to say good-bye to their father.

CHAPTER THIRTEEN

Guns and Arrows in the Trunk

The car ride back home was mostly silent. It was a Saturday morning, and Blaine and Leo's friends were probably all out playing. Leo hoped no one would see them coming home.

Blaine occasionally remarked about some fancy cars he saw or weird hairdos on some of the riders in the cars they passed, but as usual, the ride home was somber. The trunk was full of treasures, and the boys were happy to have them, but they were never quite enough to ease the pain and sorrow of saying good-bye to their father. Leo's throat tightened, and his heart beat a little faster as they turned down Fourth. Just one street more, and he would be staring at Lakeside Drive.

As the boys' father turned the big Cadillac down toward their street, Leo could see what he hoped he would not. All the kids were out, and the Cadillac immediately drew the attention of the kids who were across the street in the field. The kids came running, because they knew it meant Leo and Blaine were inside.

"I think they like your car, Dad," Blaine said.

"Yeah, they probably do. Maybe someday I can take some time to give them all a ride."

"Oh, can you do that now, Dad?" Blaine got excited at the idea of treating his friends to a ride in his dad's car. It would be a treat most of the kids would be thrilled about.

"I'm sorry, Blaine, but I really should get back up the freeway. There are lots of people heading back home after vacation, and it makes for a long drive. We still need to unload your Christmas presents out of the trunk."

Blaine pushed the button to lower his window. "Frank! Louis! We're in a Cadillac!" Frank, Louis, and the others ran alongside the car as it turned onto Lakeside Drive and pulled into a spot in front of Blaine and Leo's house. Blaine gave high-fives to the small horde of kids who nudged and pushed at each other to get a look inside the fancy car.

"Hey, little man, nice ride!" Louis yelled approval to Leo as he spotted him inside.

Leo choked up but managed to glance Louis's way. "Hey, Louis, pretty nice, huh?" He barely spoke loud enough to be heard with all the commotion caused by the other kids.

"You're riding in style, little man."

Leo smiled despite feeling torn up inside. He would wave good-bye to his father in just a few minutes, and he wouldn't be able to keep himself from crying. He knew he wouldn't be able to keep the tears in. He would feel embarrassed in front of his friends.

"All right, kids, move out of the way for a minute. I can't even open the door." The brothers' father gave gentle instructions to his sons' friends. As a father, he took pride in the greeting his boys got. He was happy to see his sons were so well-liked. He wanted to get his trunk unloaded but was patient with the throng of kids who mobbed his car.

"Okay, guys, give me a little room. Blaine and Leo have some things in the trunk. Who wants to help me carry things inside?" The boys' father directed the kids to the back of the car. He had already popped the trunk, and some of the kids stared into the deep trunk that was filled with treasures and toys for Leo and Blaine.

"Oh, yes, new bats!" one of the boys yelled.

"I hope you got a left-handed mitt, 'cause I could share that with you, Leo," another boy commented.

"Is that a bow and arrow set? Oh, man, it's got real arrows. Let me carry that!"

"A machine gun! Blaine, you guys got machine guns?" Frank was beside himself with excitement as he saw the guns being pulled out of the trunk.

"Yeah, they make real gunfire sounds, too." Blaine was out of the car and approving of the kids who were carrying off the toy treasures his father had given to him and his brother.

The mob of kids, along with Blaine, moved with the toys onto the lawn and up the walk to the front door. Blaine opened the door and let the kids all stream inside.

"Hey, everyone, not too loud; my mom's probably sleeping," Blaine said as he realized he probably shouldn't have let everyone in.

"Just set everything right over there next to the couch." Blaine pointed at the couch, but the kids already dropped things all over the living room. Leo had not yet stepped out of the car, but all the kids had left. His dad noticed he was still sitting inside, and he jumped into the back seat and sat next to Leo. Leo looked up at his dad, and tears started pouring down his checks.

"Oh, Leo, it's all right." Leo's dad grabbed a hold of him and held him tight as Leo sobbed. "Don't cry, son, or you're going to make me cry, too. We can't have grown men crying. That just wouldn't be right." His father held Leo and let him cry some more. His own eyes misted up a bit, but he willed himself to be strong and tried to focus on other things. "Leo, remember—I will be back in the summer. We'll have some more fun then. You have your school and your great friends. They all want to play with your nice things. It looks like you have some really nice friends to play with." His dad tried to control his own emotions and hoped to get Leo's mind off his sadness.

Leo wiped his face and sighed. "I know, Dad." He knew he had to get out of the car and face his friends; that was all he could manage to say without breaking down again. Leo just nodded without looking at his father's face again. He knew that would cause more tears.

"You ready to go now?"

Leo nodded.

"Okay, let's get before those kids break all your nice new things."

As Leo followed his father out of the back seat, he glanced across the street and saw Amanda. She had waited for him to come out of the car.

Leo normally would have been happy to see her, but he felt embarrassed. Amanda must have known how he felt, because she gave a quick wave but said nothing. Leo waved back and turned to walk to the front door. He quickly wiped his face again. With his head dipped low, he walked across the grass, hoping his friends wouldn't know he had been crying.

Leo passed the throng in the living room and headed straight to his room. He went to the small stack of books on his headboard, picked out a book, and started reading something—anything—to take his mind away from the sadness.

Hours later, the sun had long since gone down, their friends had left, and Blaine came in to get ready for bed. He noticed Leo with his new favorite toy.

"You going to sleep with that thing, Leo?"

"I just might, Blaine. With the way my dreams are going, I might need it." Leo pulled back on the bowstring again and let go. He enjoyed hearing the twang of the string. He couldn't wait till tomorrow morning when he would go out in the field and find some targets to shoot at.

“You never told me what your dream was about the night Dad came into the room,” Blaine said, fishing for some answers.

“Blaine, I think I might be seeing angels.”

“Angels? What do you mean?”

“Not like little chubby baby angels—you know, like cartoons and stuff. I think I’m seeing powerful—like, really powerful angels.”

“You saw those in your dream, Leo?”

“I think so. I think I saw a dark angel and maybe an angel of light. I also think I saw a full-grown Nephi. He had a book. I think he was reading it. The angel that I saw—Blaine, it was amazing!”

“It was just a dream, you know, Leo.”

“Well, I’ll keep my bowstring tight just in case.”

“Okay. You do that, little brother. Just don’t be shooting anything my way, please. Good night, little brother.”

“Good night, Blaine.”

CHAPTER FOURTEEN

The Watchers Watch for Leo

Blaine stuffed the twenty dollar bill deep into his pocket. His mother was giving him instructions before sending them off to the store. She often sent them to the store to replenish her spent six-pack of diet cokes.

"You boys be back soon. And don't you drop any of those bottles on the way back."

"Yes, Mother. Come on, Leo, let's go."

"How much did she give you?" Leo asked.

"She gave us twenty dollars," Blaine answered.

"I wasn't listening. What does she want us to get, Blaine?"

"We need to get Diet Cokes, of course, some laundry soap, and some cereal."

"Cereal—what kind?" Leo asked.

"She said we could pick, but we can only get two boxes."

"*Wahoo!* I'm getting Captain Crunch! What are you gonna get, Blaine?"

"Oh, I don't know. I'll look around when we get there."

It was a couple weeks since the boys' father had dropped them back home. They were back in school and settling into their routine. Almost every day since they came back, their friends were over at their house, bugging them to come out and play. The kids just wanted to get at the fun stuff Blaine and Leo's father had given them. The realistic machine guns and the bow and arrow sets were a young boy's dream toys. Leo loved the archery set and rarely let anyone use his. He did let Amanda use it for over an hour one day out in the field. The boys gave him a lot of heat for that.

Their life was getting back to normal, and there had been no sighting of the group of teenagers since the brothers returned. Leo was very relieved about that.

"That house still gives me the creeps," Leo said as they approached the end of their street.

"The Fultons' old house? Yeah, it's weird that we never saw them again. They fly off to Hawaii; we blow up their house, and it's like they get offended or something."

"Hah, we didn't blow up their house, Blaine—and besides, what are they going to come home to? Their house is ruined."

"Yeah, I guess. Somebody's fixing it up, though." They walked past the house and never mentioned what gave Leo the creeps. They both thought about the night when Lug and Craze died in there. They knew it could have been them.

"Hey, Mr. Stewart. Is Ben home?" Blaine hollered to his friend's father, who was out in his yard, setting up a sprinkler.

"Oh, hi, boys. No, Ben's with his mother. They're at the grocery store." Ben's father waved and continued with his yard duties.

"Okay. Thanks, Mr. Stewart."

"Hey, Leo, you think you're faster than me yet?" Blaine asked.

“Today I am. I know I can beat you today,” Leo declared, full of confidence.

“Why today, little brother, are you so sure you can beat me?”

“You’ll be easy to beat today, because today you’re twenty dollars heavier than me. See ya!” With that, Leo started sprinting in the direction of the store, still about three blocks away.

“Hey, I didn’t say go!” Blaine shouted from behind, but he knew the race was on, so he started sprinting after his brother as fast as he could. The brothers were usually pretty close in speed, and Leo had a hunch he would beat his brother that day because of the surprise jump he had. They sprinted at full speed like only young, energetic boys could. They ran and played almost every day, and a three-block sprint for fun was just that—a lot of fun. They laughed, mocked each other playfully, and jabbered all the way to the store.

Most of the run was along a dirt road rarely traveled by cars. The boys dodged a few potholes and sticks along the way. They had to throw a couple sticks at a stray dog who momentarily gave them chase. The last block of the run was on the sidewalk of a paved street with a few cars driving by. The boys tired a little—mostly because they laughed so much as they continued to joke about who was the fastest, who cheated, and so on.

As the brothers entered the parking lot of the small grocery store, they broke into a full-on sprint again to get to the front door. Onlookers looked at the two fun-loving boys as they ran. Many smiled as the fun the boys had spread to their faces. The boys ran to the door, stretched their arms out in front of them, and then crashed into the market.

“I beat you, Blaine!” shouted Leo. “You are carrying too heavy of a load today, and the speed of youth was just too much for you.”

“Speed of youth my eye; you cheated,” answered Blaine. “Hey, let’s go to the butcher in the back. He has that nice cool drinking fountain.”

"Oh, man, I was thinking of that half the way up here. I am so thirsty. That dog was scary, huh?"

"Yeah, I was hoping he would catch you so I could keep going."

"You're funny, Blaine—real funny."

The boys made their way to the back of the store, where they often came to get a drink at the fountain outside the meat cutters department. They both took long, full drinks there, and when they thought they had had enough, they went back to the well and drank some more.

The boys felt great after the run and were ready to get to their shopping. They walked the aisles slowly, eyeing all of the enticing items they wished they could have. They spent some time at the candy bins. They horsed around through most of the aisles, but after about thirty minutes, they were at the checkout stand with their mom's Diet Coke and laundry soap. Leo had his box of Captain Crunch, and Blaine had chosen a box of Cocoa Puffs.

"Hey, Leo, after this, we should go visit the Shah. We haven't seen him since the explosion at the Fultons' home. He probably heard about it."

"Okay" Leo was fine seeing the Shah but hoped he didn't want to ask a lot of questions about that night at the Fultons'.

"Here's your change, dearie." The grocery clerk handed Blaine his change, and Leo grabbed the six-pack of soda and the laundry soap.

"Thank you, ma'am," Blaine responded in his typically polite manner. Leo grabbed the bag with the cereal, and he and Blaine headed out the door and down to the liquor store to go see the Shah.

There were a few teens hanging around the liquor store. As Blaine and Leo got closer, they slowed down a little. They cautiously veered out onto the parking lot to avoid walking too close to the three boys and the girl who leaned up against the store window. All four of the kids were smoking.

"*Ooh,* aren't they cool, huh, Leo?" Blaine whispered to his brother, taking care not to be overheard.

"Quiet, Blaine." Leo definitely didn't want to stir anything up with these guys. Blaine and Leo kept their eyes to the pavement as they walked past the cool teens. As Blaine grabbed the handle of the front door, one of the teens started cursing. Leo glanced quickly over but turned back again when he saw that none of the kids were looking at him. Leo's nerves were still on edge walking past any teenagers.

"Little men! You have finally returned to see the Shah, have you? I thought I would have to go hunting for you or send my two hounds to track you down." The Shah apparently had seen the boys before they got in the door and was walking in their direction.

"Hello, Shah. It's good to see you." Blaine greeted him with a handshake.

"Hello, Shah." Leo, as was his nature, kept his words few, but he was also very happy to see his friend. It was weird at times to him and his brother, but the Shah really seemed like a friend, even though he was a grown man. Leo was too young to even guess how old the Shah was, but he seemed like he was well past forty years old. He appeared to be in good shape. He wasn't slowed by age and was pretty good with a bat, as he showed Lug and the others the last time Leo was in the Shah's store. It was weird for Leo to think about Lug. At least Lug wouldn't be a threat to Leo anymore.

"Hello to you, little man. And where is your beautiful princess you brought with you last time you were here?"

Leo shrugged and shook his head. "Um, I don't know. I guess at home."

"We just came to get some stuff for our mom. Hey, do you have any old Twinkies or cupcakes?" Blaine asked.

"I do." The Shah turned and shouted at one of his sons who helped him run the store. "Johan, can you get a few returns for my little men here?"

"Yes, I will, Father. Hello, Blaine. Hello, Leo. Are you guys okay?"

"Hi!" both brothers yelled back at Johan.

"We're fine, thanks," Blaine yelled back.

"So, boys, I heard you had some trouble with those teenagers again. I know what happened. Your friends have come in to tell me the whole story a few times. I heard about the house break-in. Is it true you also got to visit with your father?"

Leo nodded and smiled.

"Yeah, we did. It was great," Blaine answered.

"Frank and Louis told me one of the kids who was in here and chasing you, died during the fire on your street. Is that true?"

"Yeah, that's part of what happened. It was kind of scary that night, huh, Leo?" Blaine looked over at his brother, but Leo wasn't enjoying the direction the conversation was going. Blaine looked up at the kind liquor store owner.

"Leo doesn't like to talk about this stuff too much. We got to go visit our dad for Christmas vacation, but while we were there, we saw some teenagers dressed just like the guys who came in your store that night. He's having more dreams about this stuff, too." Blaine looked at his brother. "Sorry, Leo, but I think maybe the Shah can help."

Leo didn't answer; he just dipped his eyes and chin lower than they already were.

The Shah came up to Leo and gently grabbed both sides of the boy's face with his big, calloused hands. Those hands practically swallowed up Leo's whole head, but it comforted him to be held in such strong and stable hands.

"My little man, you do not need to fear what those teenagers will do, and you do not need to fear what you are seeing in your dreams. There are many who are watching out for you Leo. You have good friends, a good brother, and you have the Watchers, who will protect you."

Leo's eyes locked with the deep brown eyes of the Iranian. The lines and cracks on the man's kind face spoke of years of experience and wisdom. He smiled down at Leo.

"Watchers—I think I've read something about Watchers. How can you be sure I will be protected?" Leo asked the kind old man.

"My little men, both of you should be playing and eating Twinkies and doughnuts and never worrying or hearing of such things. It should be the concern of others." The Shah was hoping to still the fears in his young friends.

"But, they seem to know me—or that's what Lug made me think. He said the Nephi wanted to meet me or see me—something like that. Do you know what this Nephi is, Shah?"

"The boy, Lug, who died—he mentioned something about the Nephi to you, did he?"

"Yes," Leo said.

"You do not need to fear him. The Watchers know about him, and they also watch for you. You have no need to fear this Nephi. He is but a youth."

"You know about this Nephi?" Leo was surprised.

"I do know about him. He is not the only one, but this one here is only young, and his stupid teenager followers are just fools. Now two of those foolish boys have gotten themselves killed. There will be more deaths if they are not careful."

"How do you know about this stuff, Shah?" Blaine asked. He was also very surprised to hear the Shah talk about these things like this.

"I know many things, Blaine—but no more questions of such things. Enjoy your treats, and enjoy the rest of your day. I don't want you to be concerned with these things."

"But, I have so many more questions." Leo pestered the Shah. "I have dreams; can you tell me what they mean? I have seen things, and I wonder if they are real—or are they just bad dreams? Things are coming out of my dreams now."

"I know, little man; this is known. Nothing escapes the vision of the Watchers—even your dreams. Please trust me now, and think no more on these things today. Go now! Have fun like little boys are supposed to. Run hard and laugh; forget these things for now." The Shah put a firm hand on Blaine and Leo's shoulders and walked them to the door.

The teenagers were still outside to the left.

The Shah whispered to the boys, "Now look, boys, these teenagers are nothing to fear—neither are the other ones, with their dark clothing and evil plans. You go and enjoy your day."

"Thanks, Shah," both boys responded.

"And thanks for the Twinkies, too," Blaine added.

"You're welcome, and remember to come back soon."

CHAPTER FIFTEEN

Gaderel Taught Them Swordplay

"So, are they good or bad?" Amanda asked.

"It seems they can be both. I guess they were all good—or supposed to be good—but some of them chose a bad path."

Both Leo and Amanda were in the library again. They were surrounded by a large stack of books and old magazine articles. This time, though, they refused the help of the librarian's assistant. She seemed too interested in helping them, and Leo was suspicious of her behavior the last time she helped them.

"They chose a bad path?" Amanda stopped looking at the book in front of her and looked over at Leo with a puzzled stare.

"Or lots of bad paths, really," Leo added. "They were powerful and chose to go the way of Grigori."

"Um, from what I've read, some think they are still powerful. I mean, if these things were real," Amanda corrected herself. "What's Grigori?"

"I think it's a word the ancient writings used for *evil;* but in another book, it says it was the name of bad angels."

"You mean the bad angels and not the good ones who are in heaven?" Amanda asked, as she was learning stuff about angels she was never taught in church.

"Amanda, do they ever talk about these bad angels in church?" Leo asked.

"No, never, Leo. We don't know how much of this is true, but a lot of this stuff is never talked about. There are lots of angels in the stories though."

"In Sunday School, the stories have angels in them?" Leo asked.

"Yes, lots of times." Amanda eagerly told Leo what she knew. She had been able to get Leo to come to church a few times but had hoped he would start coming every week.

"What do the angels do in the stories?" Leo asked.

"Well, um, like in the Christmas story, there is the angel Gabriel. He is a mighty angel who is with God in heaven usually, but he comes to bring a message from God. There was an angel who came to a man named Gideon. And there was an angel who came and released a man from prison. And . . ."

"Okay, okay, I get it. It sounds like there are lots of angels in the stories, huh?"

"Oh, lots, Leo. They are God's messengers and servants. I so want to meet one someday when I go to heaven. I have always thought they would probably be so beautiful." Amanda had a distant look in her eye as she daydreamed of meeting the angels of her dreams.

"But what about these stories of bad angels we see here in these books?" Leo asked her. "Have you heard stories of them?"

"I don't remember ever hearing any of this at church, Leo."

"So do you think these are real?" Leo asked.

"Oh, I hope not, Leo. These sound scary to me. I just hope they aren't real."

"Me and Blaine saw the Shah the other day."

"Oh, he is such a nice man, I like him." Amanda said.

"I do too, Amanda. He said some stuff that surprised me. He said something about Watchers to me."

"Watchers?" Amanda asked.

"Yeah, he said they were watching and saw the teenagers and he said they were stupid to be doing what they were doing," Leo answered.

"Leo, we shouldn't call people stupid!"

"I know. I'm sorry, but that's what the Shah said. It sounded funny hearing an adult call the kids stupid, but that's what he said."

"*Hmm.* What else did he say about the Watchers?"

"He said they would protect me. He said they even knew about my dreams. It sounded so true to hear the Shah say that to me."

"That does sound like an angel. They watch over us—and even when we sleep, Leo."

"He mentioned the Nephi—the Shah did. He said not to worry about this Nephi, because he is young. That was just the strangest thing he said. I almost think the Shah is an angel or something. He knows so much, and when he talks, I believe what he says."

"Well, Leo, I do believe in God, and I believe in his angels—and they are powerful—but this other stuff is just too scary for me to think about."

"You are right about that, Amanda. This is pretty scary stuff here. Did you see what some of these angels taught the people?"

"No, I didn't see that. What did they teach them?"

"It says this Yeqon led all the other angels to go down and deceive the people. Another guy named Gaderel taught the people how to make swords and shields and taught them how to go to war."

"Wow, how's that make you feel about playing army now?" Amanda chided him.

"It's still fun, but it's creepy to think some angel taught humans to make weapons. Some of the other stuff that they taught I won't even say, but there is a whole list of names and the things they taught the people."

"Gosh, Leo, that must have really hurt God's heart, don't you think? He made all these beautiful people and this world with all the gorgeous animals and plants. He made these incredible angels with such power, and they go and mess things up."

"If God is so powerful to make all this, do you think things got too out of control for him?"

"No, Leo; nothing is outside of God's control. That I do know. He's too big and powerful. But he gave people free choice, and I guess he gave angels free choice, too—and this is what happens."

"Hah, look at you! You're just trying to get me to go back to church again, huh?" Leo said.

"No, but that would be nice. Can you come again soon? Please come with me again, Leo." Amanda reached over and squeezed Leo's hand. Leo blushed and used his other hand to wipe his suddenly heated face.

"Yeah, I guess so, but can I ask them about this Nephi guy who wants me to come to his meeting?"

"Ah, no, you probably shouldn't mention him." Amanda laughed loudly and then quickly covered her mouth as she looked around sheepishly.

"Um, one more thing, Amanda."

"Yes?"

"Did you read about the things called Nephilim when you were researching?"

"Yes, I did."

"You saw where they came from then, I guess?"

"Yes, it reminded me of Hercules or some of the mythical stories of the past."

"Okay, but the Shah told me this Nephi here in our town is a young one. After reading this here, it makes me wonder . . . is this happening all over again? And if it is, why am I dreaming about it? And why am I seeing my dreams in real life?"

"Is what happening again Leo?" Amanda asked.

"The Hercules thing you called it," Leo said. "the mixing of gods and humans into some sort of super creatures."

"I don't know, Leo; I don't know. That seems a bit too crazy for me to believe." Amanda patted his hand. "But the Shah said the Watchers are protecting you, and I do believe you have a guardian angel. The Bible says angels who are in the throne room of God also watch over children."

Leo appreciated Amanda's effort to comfort him, but the idea of a guardian angel always made him think of pudgy little babies with wings. They didn't seem like much protection.

CHAPTER SIXTEEN

The Sons of Darkness Send Their Dogs

"Commm, batta, swing!" Blaine yelled at Eric as he stood at the plate.

From his place at short stop, Frank took a quick glance at the guys in the outfield to see how they were playing him. Tim, on the right, was too shallow.

"Tim!" Frank yelled out. "Get deeper; he can go the other way with this. Leo, back him up if Eric goes deep!"

"Got it, Frank!" Leo yelled back at Frank from his place in centerfield. Leo held the deepest position in the outfield with Eric up. Eric was a slender kid, but with his picture-perfect swing, he could usually get good wood on the ball. He could beat out a bunt or drive the ball deep over the outfielders' heads, so everyone had to be on their toes when he was up to bat.

The Lakeside Drive kids were playing a group of kids from a few blocks over on Cloverdale Drive. There were lots of kids who lived on both streets, and they often challenged each other in various sports throughout the year. Eric volunteered to play for the Cloverdale kids, since they were one short of having nine players.

Ralphy sent his best fastball toward the ready Eric. *Crack!* Eric laced a ball that screamed over the head of Blaine, who was playing first base. It turned a little as it headed toward the right field corner and landed just outside the foul line.

"Foul ball!" Blaine yelled.

"Tim, I told you he can go in that direction, so be ready!" Frank again yelled out instructions to his right fielder. Tim was already running over to retrieve the foul ball to throw it back to Ralphy.

Ralphy caught the incoming throw on two bounces and turned to face Eric again. He looked at Eric over the top of his glove, held the ball steady as he fixed his grip, and readied another fastball. He glanced back to see that Tim was in place and ready. He looked at his catcher, nodded his head, and let go with another fastball.

Crack! Eric had timed it right and sent the ball deep.

"Dang, Ralphy!" Frank yelled at his pitcher.

"Go get it, Leo!" Blaine yelled as he saw the ball. He knew it was headed well over his brother's head.

"Bring it in fast, Leo!" Frank hollered as he ran out past the second base bag to serve as a relay.

From the crack of the bat, Leo saw right away that he needed to get on his horse. He sized up the trajectory of the ball, immediately turned, and started running to deeper center field. He knew the ball was hit so well that he had to try to do what even most big leaguers couldn't do very well. He would take his eye off the ball, run hard, and try to find it again as he set up deeper in center field in hopes of tracking down the long fly.

Leo and his brother loved to listen to Dodger games. They learned a lot about baseball by listening to the famed announcer, Vin Sully. Leo imagined himself running back into the depth of Dodger stadium and

Vin Scully calling the play as he tracked the ball to the deepest part of the field. Leo turned to try to catch the flight of the ball, and continued running. He turned again to look over his right shoulder, stretching his glove over his head and as far out as he could. In full sprint, he made a catch that would have made Willy Mays proud.

Nice catch, Leo, he thought to himself. Leo held his glove up high and spun around with a huge grin on his face as his teammates erupted with shouts and hoots. He trotted back to his regular depth in center. He was enjoying the applause and the acclaim of his friends.

"Gotcha, Eric!" Leo shouted to his friend as he enjoyed the stunned look on Eric's face. He thought for sure he had a homer, but Leo stole another one from his buddy.

"Nice catch, Leo. I guess I'll just have to hit it farther next time."

"Leo, look out!" Blaine yelled at Leo.

Puzzled, Leo looked at his brother, who was waving franticly and pointing.

"Who's that?" Tim yelled from right field. Just as Tim said that, Leo was bull-rushed to the ground. A mob of teens ran up behind him and slammed him hard on the outfield dirt. His face was forced into the gravely soil, and he felt the hands and feet of several people on his back.

"Hey, get off of him!" Blaine yelled as he sprinted to the scene where his brother was being attacked. Immediately, most of the other kids ran to the scene also. Some kids held back from fear of the large group of teens who had suddenly appeared in their friendly game of baseball.

Eric, Frank, and Louis were quick-thinking enough to grab bats before they sprinted to the mob of teens. When the three arrived with their bats, Blaine had already been thrown hard to the ground by a couple of big, broad-shouldered teenagers who met his rush to rescue his brother. One of the big kids was about to kick Blaine as Frank came upon him.

"I will bust your head, guy!" Frank yelled at the teen. He held his bat high to his right side as though getting ready to belt a fastball. The teen held back his foot and thought better of kicking Blaine.

Frank saw that Eric and Louis were at his sides, so he took a couple more steps toward the teens who had shoved Blaine to the ground. "Blaine, get up. I'll keep my bat dialed in on this creep." Blaine leaped to his feet and stood ready for any lunges from the bigger kids.

"I'll take that bat out of your hand and beat your head with it, little kid," another teen called from the pile of bodies that was on top of Leo.

"What are you guys doing, jumping on my brother?" Blaine yelled over at the kid who had spoken up.

Most of the kids who were playing baseball had gathered in a small cluster away from the scuffle. A few more brought some of the bats, as they saw there might be a need for them.

"It's none of your business, little boy," The teen called over. He spoke in a measured and steady tone, expecting the younger kids to accept and fear the unspoken threat that came with it.

"He's my brother, so it's all of my business!" Blaine was hot. He looked back at the cluster of boys and yelled out to his friend, "Spitwad, bring me that," indicating the bat in Spitwad's hand. Spitwad was a kid who lived on Lakeside Drive, but had come from Alabama and had been taught to chew tobacco by his dad. His habit of spitting his chaw gave his buddies an idea for a nickname. The name Spitwad stuck with him.

As Spitwad brought the bat and handed it to Blaine, three more kids came with him. Seven kids with bats threatened to use them on the group of teens who had jumped onto Leo. Leo was still face-down in the dirt and feeling the weight of one of the kids who sat on him. The kids had his right arm pulled up behind his back, forcing Leo in a tight, chicken wing hold that held him firm to the ground. He breathed in short breaths as he struggled with the dirt and small stones that were pressed into his left check and lips.

The two teens who had pushed Blaine felt threatened by the seven younger kids who were armed with bats. The kids looked like they could handle the bats, so the teens backed away toward their group.

"Look, you kids. We are going to take your little friend here for a little walk, and we'll bring him back to his mommy when we're done."

"You ain't going nowhere with my brother!" Blaine shouted at the whole group as he looked around and let them all know he meant business. He stepped toward the mob, and Frank and the others stepped with him, their bats held in ready position. "What do you want with my brother, anyway?"

"You guys crossed us once, and we won't forget that. Plus the Nephi wants to meet your little brother for some reason. After he is through with him, we'll send him home. Of course, he'll need to change his diaper after meeting the Nephi—right, guys?" He laughed hard and turned to his companions as they all laughed along with him.

"I'm telling you now, you ain't going nowhere with my brother. I will break this bat over your head if you try to take him. You can try to get it from me, but I'll crush your hands with it. My brother is going home with me right now, so get off him. Who wants to get hit first?" Blaine was so mad that his face was red. His friends were surprised at his fury, but the other six who held bats were fired up and at his side, ready to start swinging. They could see the hesitation in the eyes of the group of teenagers. "Get off my brother now, and send him over here!"

"Let him up." The teen who seemed to be in charge ordered the boy who held Leo to let him up. "You don't understand, kid. The Nephi asked us to bring a kid to him, and we mean to bring him a kid—do you understand?" He stared at Blaine with an intensity that shook Blaine a little.

Leo got up and ran behind his seven bat-wielding friends. Eric whispered something to him and checked on his wounds.

"Well, we want to thank you for offering to come and play baseball with us, but I think we're through now, and we will all go home," Blaine sarcastically spat back in response.

The younger kids, who were standing at a distance, were getting scared. They heard the threat about bringing a kid, and all of them were already walking or drifting farther away. All were leaving except Spitwad, who—though he was all elbows, kneecaps, and bones—was as feisty and proud as Frank and very willing to mix it up with anyone. He joined the others with a bat of his own.

"I'll just lay one of these sweet lumbers up side yo head, brothers, if you come messin' with me—ya hear?" Spitwad had a toughness that came with mixing it up in junior rodeos back home in 'Bama and wasn't afraid of some big-talking teenagers.

"Well, I guess you'll make this hard on yourselves, then." The leader of the mob reached into his pocket and pulled out a small, silver object that the friends didn't recognize. He put it in his mouth and appeared to blow into it—but there wasn't any sound.

Leo and his friends looked at each other, puzzled, and then Frank spoke up. "Oh, crud!" He pointed in the distance, where he could see three black Dobermans in full sprint, heading their way. "Run!" Frank yelled, and all the kids sprinted away from the dogs that were still a good distance away but gaining fast.

Leo and his friends made a mad dash toward the dugout in an attempt to run through the gate. They slammed the gate closed but didn't risk the time to make sure it latched. They kept running, leaving behind their mitts and the other baseball equipment. Those who had bats still held them tight.

Everyone ran as hard as they could, not even bothering to look behind for fear of seeing a snarling Doberman breathing down their necks.

Something about Dobermans struck fear in lots of kids. They were the typical junkyard dogs and had the reputation of being too vicious to mess with. Leo and his friends didn't want to find out just how vicious the dogs were. They ran hard all the way up to Lakeside Drive and up the street. Even the kids from Cloverdale ran with them.

"Let's get to my house, and my dad can call the police!" Frank looked back and yelled to all who were running with him. The mass of eighteen kids, ages eight to twelve, drew attention from some of the people who watched them run into Frank's house.

"Dad! Call the police!" Frank yelled for his dad as all the kids piled into the house and finally exhaled and felt some relief at being safe inside.

"Whoa! That was close." Eric was barely breathing and seemed to have enjoyed the little run from danger.

"We shoulda swatted those devil dogs with our bats, Frankie," Spitwad called.

"Don't call me Frankie, Spitwad, and we didn't want to have to deal with those dogs and those big kids, too. Sometimes it's best to get out safe."

"Is everybody here?" Leo looked around as he asked.

"Blaine? Hey, where's Blaine?" Leo didn't see his brother and ran to the door to check outside. He didn't see his brother there, so he ran to the edge of the grass and called for Blaine.

Frank and the others ran out with him, and the murmuring became contagious. They asked each other about Blaine and who saw him last. They all came to the dreaded conclusion that none of them could remember seeing Blaine running with them. He wasn't with them, and they knew the only place he could possibly be was back where they had just run from.

They've got Blaine! They've got my brother. Leo's brother was gone. Leo had to go rescue Blaine, just as Blaine had rescued Leo.

CHAPTER SEVENTEEN

A Return to the Dark Building

Leo fumed anxiously in the corner of the room. He was back in the Hernandez home after a very restless night at his own home. He couldn't get used to sleeping in his own bunk all night with his brother out in who-knew-where.

Many police had come and gone. It was over eighteen hours since they were first called to Frank and Louis's home. Frank's dad had called and told them what they knew. The police had interviewed all of the kids several times, with many of the officers asking the same questions over and over.

Leo was tired and angry about telling the police he didn't know the teenagers. He didn't do anything to make them mad. They had no reason to be playing tricks on each other. His brother had not run away. Leo didn't understand why they kept asking that question. *Why would Blaine run away?* His mother had insisted she had to go back to work. Leo didn't understand that, either. He was mad about that. His brother was gone, his mother was at work, and the police were still working on theories about what happened.

Leo and his friends had told the police what happened. He was furious that they weren't out looking for Blaine. The police spent time in the homes of each of the children and at the scene of the baseball game the day before. The bats that were brought back were taken to the police station as evidence.

Leo was tired from getting barely any sleep the night before. He had gone home, but a police officer had spent the night in the living room to report on anything that happened. Leo tried to sleep. Every time he dosed off—even a little—he dreamt of dark teenagers, dark angels, and huge, ugly men that haunted his attempts at sleep. He had startled himself and the police officer when he stumbled out to the refrigerator around 2:00 a.m. He was thirsty and wanted a drink, but the officer was so startled that she insisted he head back to bed immediately.

Leo listened to the various conversations and phone calls. There was a crazy buzz of activity, with people coming and going. One of the officers paced back and forth while speaking heatedly with someone on the phone. "Sir, we have gone over that with all of them already. We are not getting any inconsistencies. They are sure he was taken by these teenagers they have told us about."

Leo looked up at the blond-haired man who was looking out the open door as he stood in the entryway of the house. He wore the typical police uniform with the thick Batman-like utility belt. The belt held clubs and flashlights and a big, scary-looking gun. Leo had never been so close to so many guns before. They made him nervous; but at the same time, he knew he was safe. Those guns and clubs would protect him and his friends. It was his brother who he was concerned about. He remembered the night Lug and about twenty other teens had him, his brother, and their friends cornered in the Fultons' house. If not for a fluke fire and explosion, he and his brother could have been hurt badly that night.

Distress overwhelmed Leo again, as he knew this wasn't a dream anymore. His brother really was gone. He was safe with all these police officers, but Blaine was somewhere . . . where, he didn't know. *They've got him. Those teenagers have Blaine somewhere. I need to find him.* Somehow, Leo knew that the teens had gotten to Blaine while they were running. Blaine must have tripped, or they never would have caught him.

Leo's emotions grabbed a hold of him again. He tried but couldn't stop the tears that formed in the corners of his eyes, and escaped to run down his cheek. He dipped his head and brought his arms up to cover his face and hide his pain.

"Sir, yes, we are in close proximity, but do you think it's worth the time, sir?" Leo could still hear the police officer talking to someone on the phone. "Sorry, sir. I don't mean to question you, but I was only asking . . . you say there was a report coming in about that building?" Leo wiped his face and looked up at the officer. "Yes, sir, I believe I have a couple officers I can break away to go take a look. You say the report came from the neighbors across from the abandoned furniture building on Ford?"

The officer paused again to get more details from his superior. Leo knew the building he was referring to. It was an old building that Leo and his buddies had used on occasion for target practice. They threw rocks at the windows and doors. It had been several years since the owners had gone out of business. Leo and his friends never went inside. The building was too scary-looking, with all the broken windows and smashed-in doorways. Homeless people lived there. Leo saw them at times. They never said much, but the sight of them always scared Leo.

Leo had an idea. He popped up and scrambled outside to find Louis. Leo spotted him over by the big tree in his front yard, talking to a bunch of the neighbor kids. Leo wiped his face one more time in hopes of erasing the trail of tears. "Louis!" Leo called as he jogged over to where his friend stood.

"Leo, they done took all of our bats!" Spitwad drawled. "Man, I am so sorry for your bro. We will help you find him and pound some teenager head when we do."

"Hey, Spitwad, thanks." Leo paused and pursed his lips as he held back another rush of tears that wanted to come out. He breathed deeply, looked away, and after another deep breath, spoke to his friends. "I just heard one of the police saying they are going to check the old furniture building down on Ford Street."

"What for?" Louis demanded.

"I don't know. Maybe they think my brother's inside. Louis, would you go with me to check it out? They won't want us to go, but they can't stop us. We can sneak over there and see what's going on."

"We're there! I'll get my brother and round up the guys. I'll be back here in five minutes." Louis looked over at Spitwad. "Spit, you go get Eric. I'll find my brother. Go now."

"I'm on it, brother. We are going to rustle up some doggies. *Who-ee!*" Spitwad yelped and hollered as he ran up the street to find Eric and anyone else who wanted to go on an adventure.

Louis turned to his good friend, Leo. He was full of fun and games, always shooting off his mouth with prideful boasts—but at that moment, Louis rested his hand on his Leo's shoulder. "Don't worry, Leo. If Blaine is in that building, we will find him. He's fine still, man. You know your brother; he can take care of himself."

Leo kept his thoughts and fears to himself. He knew his brother was no match for a bunch of angry teenagers if they wanted to do him harm. Leo just hoped they had no intention of harming him. Leo hoped they were doing this to get at him. *Why do they want to get to me?* He didn't know the answer to that. He didn't know the answer to a lot of questions he had. These teenagers, his dreams, and the mysterious Nephi—among other things—still puzzled him and haunted his thoughts.

"Go find Frank, and let's go get Blaine out of there." Leo told Louis. His loyal friends gave him hope they would get his brother out of that building. *Wait . . . is something familiar about this?*

"I'll be right back, Leo." Louis encouraged his friend and ran up the street and to the right.

The kids got to the abandoned building about a half hour later. Six kids, each on a bike, raced each other to cover the six blocks where they hoped to find Blaine. They parked their bikes in the bike rack in front of the two-story apartment building across from the old Spencer's furniture store.

Leo couldn't escape the thought that dawned on him on the bike ride. He was living out one of his dreams. Months ago, he dreamt of the darkened building he entered to try to rescue his brother from his captors. That was a dream, but now he stood across the street from a building in which he believed his brother was held captive. This time, though, he stood side by side with five loyal friends. Of that he was very grateful.

Leo looked at his friends. Frank and Louis, the fiery set of brothers who lived next door, stood to the right of Leo. Spitwad and Eric were next to them. Eric was a great athlete, but his humble nature always had a calming influence on everyone. He would be emotionally steady through anything. Spitwad was another story. He was easily fired up and excitable. He would charge into anything without fear, but that could get him and others into trouble. Amanda was close to Leo, on his left. She had just come back from church with her family when the boys got on their bikes. She insisted that she come with them. Leo was especially glad to have her there, because next to Blaine, Amanda was his closest friend.

It was almost noon on Sunday afternoon. In Leo's dream months ago, he stood facing a mysterious building in the middle of a dark and rain-drenched street. A few stars peeked through the scattered clouds that were still spread out in the night sky.

This time, though, he stood with friends under a bright, cloudless sky. The sun shone bright, and the effects of the heat could be seen on the street. Small, barely visible wisps of smoke rose from the black asphalt. It had a mirage-like effect as the small amount of moisture in the street was drawn up to the sky by the heat of the sun. Leo wondered at this little scientific marvel. There were no clouds in the sky, the noontime sun was hot, and he could see in those little wisps of condensation that rose from the street the beginning of a collection of clouds that would amass somewhere above the earth.

Leo often marveled at what his school books called the laws of science. Amanda had always told him it was God, not laws of science, that caused these little marvels. Leo wished he was sitting in the library with Amanda instead of facing a nightmare scenario come to life. He thought about Amanda's faith in a God she could not see. He wanted to believe like she did, but he still had doubts about some of what she believed. He could sure use the help of a great big God who helped the little boy named David in one of the Bible stories he had heard at Amanda's church.

Leo had started to see magnificent and powerful creatures in his dreams. He wondered if they were angels. He saw good ones and bad ones. On the night Lug died, Leo saw a brilliant light shining outside of the Fultons' home just before the explosion. He didn't have an answer to what that was. He still hadn't told anyone about it. Leo had begun to wonder if that light was from some angel that saved him and his friends.

Leo glanced again at his friends, who awaited his move. They all looked a little nervous. He felt very nervous. Leo wanted help—more than just these good friends. If they went forward, would they have the help of the brilliant light creature he had started seeing in his dreams? He hoped so. He tried to imagine himself as little David. In the story, little David ran to face his giant. Leo was almost ready, but he wouldn't run like David. In his dream, he couldn't be sure why, but he knew his brother was in the building, and he had to go in to get Blaine out. Leo felt the same way now.

"Well, shall we go for a visit?" Leo looked at his friends, feeling more confident than he should have felt.

"Let's just go to the front door and see if anyone is home." Eric offered his simple approach to getting inside.

They all took a step off the curb, and as they did, they instinctively looked both ways before crossing. When they looked down the street to their right, they saw cars screaming around the corner.

The police were coming.

CHAPTER EIGHTEEN

The Roar of the Nephi

Four police cars rounded the corner and made their way down the street.

"The cavalry has shown up. We're saved!" Louis snidely remarked as the four cars pulled up to the front of the old Spencer's furniture store.

"Okay, guys. They will get the front; we should head to the back." Frank said. "Let's hustle! The police will be going in the front and will get the attention of anyone who might be inside. Let's go."

All the kids felt a whole lot better with four police cars and all the radio backup they needed close by. They raced through the filthy alleyway that led to the back side of the building. Spitwad couldn't resist kicking over one of the stinky, overstuffed trash cans as they ran past them. The sound clambered and echoed off the walls of the buildings.

"Spitwad! Knock it off!" Frank stopped and yelled at Spitwad, trying to speak as quietly as he could.

"It was in my way, man," Spitwad protested.

"Let's just keep going, guys," Eric put in, trying to keep the group calm and moving.

The others just shook their heads and headed to the back. Several years ago, deliveries took place there. The alleyway led to an intersection that crossed into another back alley street. The group turned left up that narrow street and came to the small entry door that the employees used to receive deliveries and check in for work each day.

Leo's confidence wavered a bit as they walked up the three steps that led to the door. Squarely in the middle of the door, where a knocker would be, was a small, rounded stone with three letters in the middle—*sod.* It was all too familiar for Leo. He believed he knew what the letters meant and what would happen when they opened that door.

"Guys!" Leo called out to his friends. "Everyone take a deep breath before we go in."

"What?" Louis asked.

"Take a deep breath—even take a couple deep breaths. The air in there might be a bit stuffy or smelly. The air out here is going to be much better than what we find inside." Leo remembered struggling to breathe inside the building in his dream. He wanted to be prepared for that.

Frank reached out to the doorknob and looked back toward everyone. "That's a good idea. Everyone take a deep breath—and Spitwad, try to keep quiet." He turned the knob and slowly pulled the door open. As he did, a cloud of smoke came billowing out. It spilled out the doorway and immediately rose into the sky. Frank had the door all the way open. The hallway before them was nearly covered in smoke. Only about four feet of clear air could be seen along the floor. The smoke lit up at times from what looked like flickers or sparks.

"Fire!" Spitwad yelled. "If Blaine is in there, we best get on in and drag him out, boys." He yelled what the others knew already. There was a fire somewhere in the building, and it looked like it was spreading fast.

The kids got down on their hands and knees and crawled further in. By using their shirts and hands, they covered their mouths and noses against the smoke that threatened to choke them and halt their attempts at a rescue. As they crawled, they coughed and gagged as they eased themselves down the hallway.

Leo, sensing he had seen this before, looked past his friends down the hallway. As he looked to the farthest point, he saw what he expected to see. In the smoky haze, he saw someone scurry from one room to another. *I know what comes next!*

"Stop!" Leo yelled at everyone. He wasn't concerned about how much noise he made. "I think they are coming from this direction." Leo pointed to the left—other than the hallway, it was the only direction in which someone could travel. "I think I hear them; they might be bringing Blaine." He was lying. He didn't hear anyone but was trying to learn from what he had dreamt. "Let's get back toward the door—and quick."

Leo's friends didn't understand his reasons, but they followed his lead and turned to crawl back toward the door. As they made their way to the door, they heard a scramble of feet to the right.

"Let's hurry to the doorway," Leo whispered.

"Who's that there?" someone in the direction of the scuffle yelled out. The kids knew they had been spotted. Just then, they heard approaching sirens. The fire had apparently been spotted and called in—probably by the police out front. Leo's heart raced as he and the others crawled faster toward the door.

From where an obvious scuffle of feet and a struggle of bodies could be heard some yards away in the thickening smoke, a shocking roar sounded, as if a huge lion was ready to pounce on its prey. The kids froze in stunned silence as the roar shook the walls with its thunder. They were too scared to move for fear the lion would see them and give chase. It roared again, and Leo began to shake in fear. *He's coming for me.*

The smoke filled his lungs and made it hard to breathe, plus the fear of the unseen lion paralyzed him. He looked down the hall, where he expected to see the lion. He could see the group he expected would be bringing Blaine. Coming out of the billowing smoke gave them a ghost-like appearance. Still too afraid to move, the six friends crowded together in a mass to await what or who was coming.

The voice called out again, "Who are you guys? What are you doing in here?"

None of the kids dared to give an answer.

Leo saw who spoke. It was one of the teenagers who was a part of the group that threatened them in the baseball field the day before. He also saw his brother. Blaine fought hard against those who held him as they dragged him through the hallway.

"That's a doorway. Let's get out!" someone in the group shouted. He must have seen the door as an escape route from the fire that raged through the hall. The spreading flames were getting bigger. The inferno could be seen running through the ceiling and walls.

Seemingly on cue, everyone sensed the growing danger and surged toward the door. The mad dash for safety propelled the kids and the teenagers toward the same small opening. Shoulders, legs, and arms jammed into each other as all the kids pushed and clawed their way through the limited opening.

As the door was flung open, more smoke was released to the outdoors. This brought more oxygen to fuel the mounting fire. The flames lashed out at the boys as they crowded through the doorway.

Many of the kids shrieked at the blast of fire that burned and singed hair and clothing. Amanda and Eric got out first, but bodies flew on top of them. Blaine was released by his fleeing captors and helped push and pull everyone out the door. He and Leo were last at the door and helped shove everyone out. The teens showed no evidence of bravery or chivalry. They made it to daylight and just kept running. Blaine and Leo struggled to help Frank out and then lunged through the doorway and toward the final three steps that led to safety.

Leo followed his brother out the doorway. He was hot on his tail when he heard the deafening roar of the lion again—right behind him. Leo spun around to face the roar as he stepped off the porch. As he spun, he lost his footing on the top step. His momentum sent him flying into the air with his back toward the ground. He was surprised to see not a lion, but the tall teenager. It was the tall kid from the fire meeting, and the one who had stopped and stared at him. It was the young Nephi.

In his fall that felt like slow motion, Leo made eye contact with the teen. The teen responded with a toothy, devious grin. He brought his foot forward to leap off the porch. His foot passed right in front of Leo's face, and he saw very clearly the split hoof of a goat at the end of the teen's leg.

The Nephi planted his hoof square on Leo's chest as he landed on the ground and pushed hard against him as he leaped away. Leo's lungs were compressed between the hoof and the ground, and he was stunned and scared at the end of his short fall. He couldn't catch his breath. He knew his breath would return again, but it was still scary.

As Leo lay there, trying to regain his breath, he thought about what he had just seen and heard. Amanda's face suddenly was in front of his. "Leo! Leo, are you all right?" Leo nodded but was unable to speak.

"Amanda, he got the wind knocked out of him. Give him a moment." Blaine was with Amanda, kneeling over Leo.

"Blaine!" Amanda screamed out his name at the sudden realization of who knelt next to her.

"Leo, it's your brother!" Amanda shouted the obvious to Leo as he lay on the ground. Leo just smiled. Air was returning to his lungs, but he wasn't yet ready to speak.

"I think he knows who his brother is, silly." Louis said and then busted into laughter as he saw the big smile on Leo's face.

"Have you had breakfast yet?" Leo asked his brother the silly question that he knew would get a silly response.

Blaine grabbed a hold of his brother's hand and squeezed hard. "No, I didn't get a chance, bro. I have been busy. Do we have any more Captain Crunch? I hope!"

The friends all laughed. Leo sat up and hugged his brother. All the friends slapped hands and hugged. The noise of Spitwad's whooping could be heard past the end of the street.

The firemen made their way toward the kids, shouting out commands to clear the area. The friends had no problem with that. They picked themselves up and skipped, scooted, and almost danced their way back to their bikes on the front side of the building.

"Well, this is starting to look familiar. Another escape by fire, huh, Leo?" Blaine high-fived his brother, threw his arm in the air, and screamed at the top of his lungs. "Thanks for coming by, guys. It's nice to see you." Blaine was very glad to see his friends after his harrowing ordeal. He let out a big sigh of relief and then sat down on the curb and watched the firemen struggle with getting a handle on the flames that raged through much of the old building.

If Not Human, Then What?

The next two days were filled with many trips to the police station. The same female police officer was again, a regular overnight guest in the boys' home. They felt better with the protection she offered, even though they hadn't asked for it.

The police recommended that the boys stay home from school for at least a week so they could more fully investigate the various stories and try to match up pictures with potential names. Leo and Blaine would have preferred being with their friends at school. They had some amazing stories to tell and only had each other to tell them to. However, the time away from school turned out to be a good opportunity for Blaine and Leo to talk about all that had happened and connect some of the events to Leo's dreams. Leo told Blaine about his dream of the dark building months ago. Blaine had never heard the details of that dream. He was blown away at hearing that his brother knew he was in the building and that the teens would drag him down the hallway when they did.

"No way. That is way too crazy, man!" Blaine exclaimed.

"It's true. As soon as I saw someone cross over down the hallway, I knew it was like in my dream. The guys were down a little in front of me. I called them back and told them we should get outside. The guys holding you spotted us before we could hide, but I just knew they would be coming, and they would have you. It's that roar, though; that's different than my dream. Nothing like that happened."

"But you said the big, ugly guy had stared into your face in your dream."

"Right, and what happened for real was the big kid who I'm sure now is what the Shah said was a young Nephi. He stared at me as I was falling backwards off the steps."

"Wow!" Blaine exclaimed. "You said the Shah told you he was a young Nephi—meaning he will probably get big and ugly."

"I don't know about ugly, but bigger, yeah—at least, that's what I think," Leo answered.

"What do you think the roar was?" Blaine asked.

"I think it came from him, Blaine—in fact, I'm sure it did."

"Why do you think it was him? He's just a big teenager, for crying out loud. He's not a lion!"

"Dude, it was right behind me—the roar, that is. I turned, and there he was. Then he leaped like some gazelle or something—and never looked back, I assume."

"Yeah, that I saw. He was like a blaze when he took off. I couldn't believe how fast he ran."

"Guess what else?" asked Leo.

"What?" Blaine responded.

"He stepped on my chest, and his foot was, like, right in front of my face." Leo paused for effect. "It was a goat hoof, Blaine. He didn't have normal feet. He had feet like a goat-man."

Blaine just stared at his brother.

"In my other dream that was more recent, the Nephi I saw had hooves like a goat or something. He was sitting in the middle of these weird creatures."

"The horse-lions, right?" Blaine asked.

"Right, but I have been calling them lion-horses. I don't know what to call them, but that just seems like what they should be called. Maybe he's related to the lion-horses somehow," Leo suggested. "Maybe that's how he can roar like that."

"Whoa, now! You think this kid isn't human—like some animal or something?"

"I'm not ready to say what he is, Blaine, but things just don't seem right, and I'm trying to figure them out."

The boys went back and forth like that for hours, sharing stories, dreams, and ideas. Blaine told Leo about his night in the abandoned building. Leo was right in his guess that Blaine must have tripped. When Blaine tripped, the teens were on him instantly. They stopped chasing the others and took him right away to the old furniture store.

Blaine didn't sleep much at all, but he told the police that the teens never hurt or threatened him. He did tell the police what Leo had feared for a while. The teens wanted Leo for something.

"They were all talking about you, bro. It must have been that every one of them was told to look for you. They knew your name, and when they would talk to me or bring me food or take me to the restroom, they would all call me Leo's brother."

"You said the tall one, the Nephi, was asking about me a lot, too?" Leo asked.

"Yeah. He sat down with me a couple times and was asking about your dreams. He wanted to know why you were in the field that night."

"Did you tell him we were just playing?"

"I did, but what's weird was, he looked at me, kind of surprised or like he didn't know what that was."

"Playing—he didn't know what playing was?" Leo was very surprised at this.

"It didn't look like he did. He was very calm all the time. He never seemed scary. Some of the other guys did, but this bigger teenager—the one you call the Nephi—he was in control, and nobody questioned him. He wouldn't let anyone come and threaten me, so I felt pretty safe most of the time."

"Huh. I wonder what they want. They never said, huh?"

"No," Blaine responded. "They just wanted to know about your dreams, and they wanted to talk with you."

"Sounds so harmless," Leo mused, "but no way I want to talk to them, Blaine."

"No, I don't think you should," Blaine agreed.

Most of the families on the block and many from surrounding streets came to visit the boys and hear some of their story. A couple local news channels got wind of the news and tried to interview Blaine and Leo. The police wouldn't allow it, and Leo was happy about that. The news had to settle for Frank, Louis, and Spitwad. Blaine and Leo got a kick out of seeing Spitwad go on television, spinning his tales about swinging bats at kids and his rodeo-days back in Alabama. The poor news anchor had trouble breaking away from Spitwad's tales. It was good for Blaine and Leo to laugh at that. They enjoyed seeing their friends on television.

Spitwad had run over to tell the brothers that he would be on the television that night. He got a stern look from the female police officer who served as the boy's bodyguard. She relented, though, and let him in for a few minutes. Spitwad thought he was a star. He enjoyed his fame.

These things humored Leo and gave him a chance to relieve some stress that had built. He slept for long, dreamless nights on Monday and Tuesday. He knew, though, that he would have to settle back into his daily routine again soon. He would have to go to school again. He would have to walk there and walk back.

The teenagers were looking for him for sure. They knew where he lived. They knew his name. They knew about his dreams—at least, the strange one called the Nephi did. *What was he? Did he make that roaring sound? He can't be human, can he? If not, what is he?* Leo knew he must talk to Amanda. She would be a big help in finding some answers.

CHAPTER TWENTY

Crossbred Leaders of the Sons of Darkness

Leo and Amanda sat in the back corner of the library on Saturday morning a week and a half after the police had finished interviewing, calling, and leaving a night watch at Blaine and Leo's home. Leo and Amanda had settled into their favorite spot. It was quiet, tucked over on one of the side walls under a row of windows. The wall rose high under a raised ceiling with the row of windows, about ten feet up, that let in the morning sun. They liked the spot, because it was away from the busier sections where kids' story centers and book-review clubs met. Leo enjoyed the sunlight that broke through in the early morning hours. Just after sunrise, the light streamed in through the windows and spilled its cheery light on the readers who were lucky enough to grab the best seats.

On that morning, Leo and Amanda waited as the doors opened. They were lucky, as usual, to be able to grab one of the bright, sunny spots in the corner. The sun warmed them as they plowed through a fresh pile of books. Leo missed out on playing football with the guys again, but there was too much on his mind with the dreams and real life getting much too close to each other and much too dangerous.

Leo told Amanda about the goat hooves on the tall teenage kid. Amanda didn't believe him at first, but after his persistence, she started to realize that the tall kid must have been more than what he appeared to be. At least, that is what Leo tried to get her to believe. Amanda and Leo searched for answers.

Leo's brother was kidnapped by teenagers who believed in and followed someone or something called a Nephi. The Shah seemed to think the stuff about the Nephi was true. Lug, though he was dead, was sure a believer in the Nephi. Leo had known something would happen in the abandoned building before it did. He knew this because of something he dreamed about. Who were the Watchers the Shah spoke about? Who or what was the bright thing that Leo saw just before the explosion in the Fultons' home? Football with the guys would have to wait a while longer.

"See? Look here, Leo," Amanda said, breaking the calm serenity of the sun-drenched reading time both were enjoying. "It shows that some creatures, called seraphim, can have six wings, or things called cherubim can have four or even six wings, and some have cow faces and lion faces."

"That is so bizarre. Cow faces, huh?" Leo asked. "Did you see the place where it said there were four special ones that had four faces to each creature? Four faces! They wouldn't ever have to turn their heads; they could see everywhere all the time."

"Yeah, that's like Mrs. Ferguson." Amanda chuckled. "She always tells us she has eyes in the back of her head."

Leo snickered at that. "Maybe she turns into one of these creatures at night. If we keep searching, we might come across her picture in one of these books." Leo got a kick out of his own joke, smiling and chuckling as he flipped some more pages.

"Leo!" Amanda shouted, immediately jabbing her finger in the place where she was reading.

"Quiet, we're in a library." Leo looked apologetically back at a few of the people he could see staring at Amanda. "What did you find?"

“You said in your dream, that guy had a book in his hand. Look at this. Right here—this creature has a book in his hand and gives it to a man and tells him to eat it.

“He eats a book?” Leo gave a puzzled glance at his friend as he took a closer look at where she was pointing.

“Now, holding that place, if I flip over here, there is this brilliant creature that is gigantic. He has a face as bright as the sun, and his feet are on fire. Are you listening, Leo?”

“Yeah, I’m right here. What do you mean?” Leo asked, confused.

“Listen to this.” Amanda read to him out of the book. “And he had in his hand a little book open; and he set his right foot upon the sea, and his left foot on the earth, and cried with a loud voice, as when a lion roars.”

Leo’s face brightened with recognition. “Let me see that.” Amanda slid the book over to him. He read it again to himself and slowly turned to face Amanda. “That’s it. He roared like a lion, just like that teenager did . . . that’s what I’ve been telling you, Amanda! According to this, these things can get big enough to stand with one foot on the sea and one foot on the land. I wonder if this lion kid I saw will get that big.”

“Now, wait a second, Leo.” Amanda held her hand out to correct him. “I don’t think these two things are the same thing. For one, I think this creature here is a good creature, but you think this Nephi is bad, right?”

“Right, I think he is, but . . .” Leo paused and thought about his words before he spoke again. “Look, Amanda, none of this should be real, but . . . it just is, right?” Amanda nodded to him, and he continued. “These things are really happening. We heard that roar. It was as real as this pile of books in front of me.”

Amanda held up her hand again to stop him. “What I’m getting at, Leo, is this—you seem to be suggesting this kid isn’t a real person.”

Leo just stared at her, and Amanda stared back. They both considered the implications of what they were thinking.

"Yes, that's what I am thinking." Leo broke the silence. Amanda raised her eyebrows and slowly shook her head with wonder.

"Okay, that's what I thought you were thinking, so let's take another look at this." Amanda grabbed another book and tugged at one of the little green tabs she had placed in it earlier. "Read that."

Leo looked at the place she had marked with sticky notes. He read and reread the two paragraphs she had marked, looked up, and took a deep breath. "So it looks like—according to this, anyway—that the Nephi could be a cross between a human and one of these creatures. He is a child of that union, and they do get big, Amanda."

"Yes, Leo, they can get big, but there are other places where this is spoken about, and they are sometimes bizarre-like and not human-like."

"So you agree with me, then, that the lion roar could have come from that kid?"

"Leo, these texts that we are looking at date back almost three thousand years. That's a long time. They must have felt pretty strongly about this stuff to write it down and protect it and continue to pass along these stories and beliefs."

"This is starting to sound like science fiction stuff, Amanda—to think they're some sort of cross-breeds. But this still doesn't answer the other questions. What is going on? What do they want with me, and what are these teenagers involved with?"

"I don't know that, Leo, but they clearly are dangerous—but this isn't something we can go to the police with. This is . . ." Amanda didn't know how to finish her thought. "You know, Leo, I didn't want to bring this up, but we never looked further into your idea about *sod.*"

"*Sod*—you mean Sons of Darkness?" asked Leo.

"Yes, that. It sounds too creepy to me, but if that is one of their names, than surely they are up to no good."

"I know. After my dreams got creepier and after hearing what the Shah told me and everything else that has happened, it's like the teens and their *sod* t-shirts are the least of our worries."

"You're probably right, Leo."

"Thanks, Amanda. You are such a good friend for helping me with this. We should go. I want to go play with Blaine and the guys if they're still out. This stuff is making my head spin anyway," Leo said.

Amanda reached over and grabbed Leo's hand. "Leo, I want to help. I don't know where this will lead us, but I will help you however I can."

Leo blushed again. He tried to hide it by getting up and grabbing at one of the piles of books.

CHAPTER TWENTY-ONE

A Smart Kid, but He's Dumb as Mud

A week had passed and Leo and Amanda were back in the library for another few hours of research. Amanda was not very happy with Leo.

"No, Leo; I won't look at those anymore. I think they are disgusting, sick, and evil!" Amanda insisted.

"But I thought you would help me find some more answers to this," Leo shot back.

"Leo, I will help you—and I have—but I am not going to look at those kinds of books anymore. Why don't we look more at the books of Enoch, Ezekiel, or the book of Jasher? They had lots of information on the angels and the ones that went bad. Those other books just make the bad angels look good. I know that's wrong, Leo."

Leo just looked away in frustration. He was irritated and upset, so he grabbed the new books and took them back to the counter for the assistant to put back. Leo turned away from the counter before walking back to the table where Amanda sat.

It was just after 10:00 on another Saturday morning, and Leo and Amanda were in their familiar spot in the library. There was a group of older men and women in the library's coffee nook, talking, laughing, and enjoying some tea and sweets. Leo imagined he would be like that someday. He figured he would always love to read, and when he got older, he would find himself in the library, drinking tea with friends. He sometimes pictured Amanda in the library with him, too—but he was too mad at her to think like that. She didn't want to look at the books the librarian's assistant brought over. He knew Amanda was probably right, but he didn't see the harm in just looking through them.

Leo started to walk back to where Amanda sat. She was wearing Levis and a red sweatshirt he liked. He thought she looked very cute in it. He always wanted to tell her she looked cute but could never get up the courage. He just called her Little Red Riding Hood and teased her about it. She got mad, and he felt awkward. He only said it because he liked how it made her look, but she thought he was making fun of her. They had that little exchange again that morning when she came over to meet him on their way to the library.

Blaine didn't help, either. He yelled out that Leo's girlfriend was at the door. Leo got embarrassed and started calling Amanda Little Red Riding Hood. The walk to the library was quiet and a bit tense. Leo figured it was his fault Amanda was mad at him. He wished he could have just said she looked cute instead of calling her Little Red Riding Hood.

"Boys! Please slow down, and watch where you are going." The librarian tersely corrected three boys who nearly bumped into Leo as they ran over to the group of first and second graders who were gathering for the morning story time.

"Sorry, Mrs. Turner." The boys slowed down and looked a little embarrassed in front of Leo.

Leo strolled over to the table where Amanda was and sat down. Amanda never looked up. She just kept her eyes glued to the book of Ezekiel she was investigating.

"I thought you didn't trust her, Leo," Amanda snapped.

"What? Who didn't I trust?" Leo defended himself.

"Her—the librarian's assistant, whatever her name is."

"Alice," Leo responded.

"What?" Amanda paused. "You know, I really don't care what her name is. That's not the point. You told me you thought she was suspicious. You said you think she had something to do with leading Lug over to our street that day. Do you remember that, Leo?"

"Yes, but I don't know that; I was just guessing."

"Just guessing; just guessing. Well, Leo, you have been just guessing about all your dreams and all this stuff that is happening. That's why we are trying to figure some of this stuff out by looking into these books. But now she is being so nice and giving you these books that are all about magic and spells and evil stuff that we shouldn't have anything to do with." Amanda took a breath and looked up at the ceiling in frustration.

"She's just trying to help," Leo meekly responded.

"Leo, you are probably the smartest kid in school, but sometimes you are as dumb as a dirt clod."

Leo returned a startled look at his friend.

"Some guy threatens me, your brother, and your friends with a knife, and we barely escape. Now because this girl wears nice perfume and is smiling at you when she brings you all those books, you forget all that. Mud, that's it—you're dumber than mud, Leo."

"I don't care about her perfume." Leo was flustered and didn't know what to say. He was a bit captured by Alice's pretty smile. Leo wondered if Amanda had noticed that. "I'm sorry, Amanda. I won't look at the books she suggests any more if that's what you want."

"Well, then take this one back, too." Amanda handed Leo another book that Alice had brought over.

"I'll be right back." Leo took the book and walked back to the counter. On his way there, he saw Alice at the end of one of the aisles. He decided he would take the book to her and explain. He sheepishly walked up to her and tapped her on the shoulder.

"Oh, hi. Did you find that book helpful?" Alice asked as she turned to look at Leo. As she did, she flipped her long blonde hair off her face. The scent of the perfume Amanda mentioned sweetly enticed Leo again. *That is nice perfume,* Leo thought to himself. Alice smiled sweetly, and Leo couldn't help staring at her beautiful, perfect teeth.

Alice could tell the young boy was captivated by her beauty. "You're cute. What's your name?"

Leo immediately blushed. He knew he had been caught staring. "Um, Leo." Leo stumbled over his name.

Alice reached for the book Leo had in his hand. As she did, she also leaned into him and gave him a quick kiss on the cheek.

Leo was ready to either melt into the floor or float away at that moment. A beautiful girl had just kissed him. He was shocked and surprised. The smell of her perfume and the soft press of her lips on his cheek were all he could think of. Her lips felt slightly moist and very soft. He stared at Alice's lips again and saw them pull back into a broad smile to reveal her perfect teeth.

"Leo . . . are you in there?" Alice sweetly and charmingly tried to pull Leo out of his trance. "The book—did you find it helpful?"

"Oh, yes, I did. Thank you for all your help." Leo was still caught in the web of her smile and the memory of the kiss on his cheek. He would have agreed to anything at that moment. He lied about the book being helpful, since he never even opened it.

"Leo, I'll see you later!" called Amanda.

The spell on Leo was immediately shattered. He turned and realized Amanda was just a few feet away. By the look on her face, he could tell she probably saw the kiss and heard the dumb response he gave while under its spell. *I am as dumb as mud.*

"Uh, you're leaving now?" Leo stammered.

"Yes, I'm done here. I left your books on the table. You can get those or let your assistant get them for you." Amanda turned and stomped toward the exit.

Leo was busted, and he knew it. He was too afraid to run after his friend, though that's what he wanted to do. The memory of Alice's soft lips on his cheek was chased off by the shame he felt. Amanda had warned him. She probably was right, but he felt stuck and embarrassed. He tried to hide his feelings from Alice.

"Oh, I'm sorry if I embarrassed you in front of your girlfriend," Alice not so slyly jabbed at Amanda, who was too far away to hear.

"Uh . . ." Leo stammered again. "She, well, isn't my girlfriend . . . she's just a really good friend. I guess I made her mad. It wasn't you."

"Will you tell her I'm sorry, please?" Alice tilted her head slightly and brushed back her bangs to try to set her spell in motion again.

"Yes, I will," Leo lied. "I guess I should go, too. I—I'm not so interested in any more research right now."

"Well, Leo, I will be glad to help you anytime you are in. I'm usually working Saturday, so maybe next week, okay?"

"Okay, that sounds good. Sorry about the books we left out."

"That's fine, Leo. I can get those put away."

Leo turned and walked toward the door. He was walking away from a beautiful girl who had just kissed him, but he was troubled by it.

Something churned inside him. The kiss made him feel amazing, but he thought that Amanda was probably right—he should not trust her. Leo walked slowly home. He didn't want to run into Amanda. He felt terrible about what happened but wasn't sure what to say to her yet.

CHAPTER TWENTY-TWO

Drawn Back to the Fire

The following day Leo was eager to make amends, and met Amanda in front of her house when she returned home from church. He hoped her time at Church would have calmed her down, but things didn't go as he would have liked, when he asked for her forgiveness.

"Yes, of course I do, Leo, but you were being really stupid, okay?" Amanda yelled at Leo.

Leo cringed at the harsh response from his friend. "You don't sound like you do."

"I do forgive you, Leo, but that girl is up to no good, and I think you should know that." Amanda was calmer, but she was still hot about seeing Alice kiss Leo after she warned him about her.

"Look, I know you're probably right . . ."

"Probably?" Amanda interrupted him in mid-sentence.

"Okay, I guess you are right, but we don't know for sure, do we?" Leo adjusted his answer, but he could see Amanda still wasn't happy with his making excuses for Alice.

"With all that's been going on lately with you, Leo, I'm surprised you're willing to take a chance."

"I'm sorry." Leo decided to change the subject. "How was church today?"

"It was good; it's always good. You should have come with me."

"Well, you didn't ask, and I figured you were still mad at me," Leo responded.

"I was, but you are always welcome to come with us to church."

"What was the story about this morning?" Leo asked.

"Samuel—it was the time when he was." She paused, and didn't finish her sentence. "Leo, you should have been there. This was the story when a little boy named Samuel has dreams, and he hears the voice of God."

"*Hmm,* the voice of God, huh? Wow! So what happened?"

"They just talked about his dream and hearing God's voice, but the point is what I was saying yesterday at the library. You don't need to go into those weird, dark books. There are stories and books that can help you find answers. There are books that don't get into that dark stuff."

"You mean the Bible?" Leo responded meekly.

"The Bible, of course, but there are other books, too, if you want more to research. There is the book of Jasher, the book of Jubilees, the book of Enoch, and there are others. There are lots of books like those that the ancient writers and scholars passed down for centuries that have been read and accepted and used by good scholars. You don't need those dark and evil books."

"Okay, I see your point." Leo was properly chastised by his good friend.

"Leo!" Blaine yelled from their front yard.

Leo turned to respond. “What do you need, Blaine?”

“Hi, Amanda. How was church?” Blaine politely remembered not to ignore her.

“Hi, Blaine. It was fun. You should come next time.”

“I would for sure, but I’m going to get my hair dyed that day,” Blaine joked.

“Liar. You should get it done in green, then,” Amanda answered.

“What did you want me for, Blaine?” Leo said.

“Oh.” Blaine jumped off the small landscape stone he was standing on and jogged across the quiet street. “I guess I don’t need to yell from across the street at you two. If you two want to come with us, we’re going to the field again tonight.”

Amanda’s face turned pale. “Blaine, I thought the police said you shouldn’t go out there for now.”

“Uh, well, we know, but . . .”

“Have you been taking some of your brother’s dumb pills?” Amanda interrupted.

“Dumb pills? So he’s not naturally dumb?” Blaine looked at his brother and smiled. “You have to take pills to be this dumb, Leo?”

“Funny, Blaine,” Leo deadpanned back.

“Tell you what—I gotta go, but if you two want to come with us, we’re going to meet in front of the old Fulton house at 7:00.”

“It’s dark by then, Blaine,” Amanda put in.

“Yes, but the boogey man comes out then, too, and we want to meet him. I’m going to go get some more guys to come, so meet us at 7:00 if you want to come." Blaine ran off up the street with Leo and Amanda watching. He stopped briefly to pet one of the neighborhood dogs who ran up to greet him. Blaine continued on his jog and turned toward Frank and Louis's house.

Amanda turned to Leo. "Are you going to go with him?"

"Yeah, I couldn't stay home if I knew him and the guys were going to be out."

"Okay, then I'll be there, too. I'm going to go home to pray for you, Leo, and your dumb pills. You should have been at church; the little boy, Samuel, heard the voice of God. You could learn that lesson yourself, Leo."

"Bye, Amanda." Leo waved at her as she turned and walked up the street to her house. He didn't mind the little barb she threw at him. He was glad she wasn't too mad at him anymore.

At 7:00, the corner in front of the burned-out house where the Fulton's used to live was full of kids. Blaine had been to every house on the street. With all the curiosity about what had been going on lately, none of the kids wanted to miss anything. Leo and Amanda were glad for the crowd, because it made them feel safer.

"At least we won't be sneaking up on anybody this time." Leo said, as he looked out into the darkened field, from the corner, in front of the Fulton's old home.

The sun had gone down at 6:15. The streetlights were on, and many stars peeked through from their distant homes in the galaxy.

There was a buzz of anxious chatter amongst the kids. Most of the Lakeside Drive kids had heard many of the stories. They knew some of the stories involved a chance encounter in the field across from the Fulton's home. From the spot where they all stood on the corner, the reason for the buzz could be clearly seen out in the field. Someone had a huge fire going in the field about a hundred yards out—just like the fateful night when Leo and Blaine stumbled upon those teens. A good number of people could be seen amongst the trees and bushes around the fire, which was out by one of several groupings of oak trees that were clustered around the field. This wasn't any secret meeting like the one Leo stumbled upon. Whatever was going on out there was out in the open after dinner time.

"Do you think it's them, Leo?" Louis asked.

"I hope it's a bunch of old ladies playing cards," Leo joked back.

"Not me. I hope it's them. With all these friends here, we'll make lots of noise," Louis countered back.

As the kids stared at the fire, a little green four-door Toyota pulled up across the street from where they stood. The back passenger door opened, and out stepped Alice, the librarian's assistant.

Amanda's jaw dropped when she saw Alice get out. Alice turned and looked at the group of younger kids on the corner. Amanda looked over at Leo, grabbed a hold of his arm, and leaned over to whisper in his ear. "Oh my gosh, Leo, what do you think she is doing here?"

Leo shrugged, and they both watched Alice as she came around the back side of the car. She stopped and said something to the driver, who then drove off. Alice glanced again at the crowd of kids. She smiled at everyone, waved, and then turned to walk into the field.

There were a few scattered trails that snaked through the field. Alice took the first one she came to. It led her right to the big group of people at the fire.

"Did she wave at us to come with her?" Leo asked.

"That's what I thought, too!" Amanda said.

"She's inviting us to follow her," Leo responded in amazement.

"Okay, since we're being invited, then maybe we should go!" Frank shouted to everyone. With his loud voice booming over the crowd of kids, everyone got quiet.

"Listen up, everyone. We're just going for a walk in the field. Nobody wander off. Let's stay close to each other. We don't know who this is over by the fire, but last time there was a fire in this field, the big kids gave us a chase for being too close to their meeting. If this is another one of those, they might not be very happy again. Let's remember to stay together, and if anyone gives us any trouble, Blaine and I will do the talking. Now let's go."

"Wahoo!" several kids shouted, excited to have a thrill of their own. The noisy group of neighborhood friends crossed the street and headed out toward the big bonfire in the middle of the field.

Arrows for the Heart of the Nephi

Leo inched closer to his target in the darkness. He could see the light of the fire up ahead. He stilled himself, listening for any indication that his approach was noticed. The sparks of the fire flew high into the forested night sky. He guessed it was probably caused by the witches who were beating at the edges of the fire and stirring the logs again. It wasn't the usual stoking of a fire typically done around a campfire. The witches Leo had seen before purposely fanned and beat the fire to cause a great flurry of sparks to follow the smoke in its ascent into the black sky.

There were no stars to be seen that night. The blanket of clouds was full of moisture and looked like it might at any moment send down another drenching. The most recent downpour had soaked the ground. Leo's shirt was soaked too, as he crawled to get closer to the fire. The bed of pine needles was soft and comfortable normally, but tonight, the moist needles made him shiver.

Leo crept closer. As he did, the sheath that held his Bowie knife caught on a root. He kept his eyes forward as he reached back with his left hand to free his knife. It would not do to lose that now. He was determined to end the life of the Nephi that night. If his arrows missed their mark, he was determined to plunge his faithful Bowie deep into its neck. He hoped his shots would be true. He knew that once he was in position, he could release three to four arrows toward his nemesis before he knew they were on their way toward his heart—if his enemy was where he expected him to be. Leo had spent too many years in training to let the Nephi get away again.

Leo eased his way closer over the soggy needles. He guessed he was about seventy five yards away. It was a perfect distance. If the Nephi was seated, as Leo expected he would be, Leo could get at least three arrows off before the first one had time to reach its mark.

His personal bowyer and he had together crafted a longbow of extraordinary strength. Leo's strength training enabled him to pull the mighty bow with ease. His years spent learning speed archery helped him master the skill. He had risen to the top of his class. His mastery of the bow was why he was chosen to hunt the Nephi.

Soundlessly, he eased himself up beside the trunk of the dual pines that stood before him. In their younger years, the two pines had started out as individual saplings, but long after, they had merged their trunks and bark. They grew as Siamese twins, merged at the hip. The trunks of the trees began to split apart about five feet off the ground. This would prove to be a perfect blind and launch point for Leo to loose his arrows toward their mark.

Leo eased his face along the bark of the trees where they split, to catch a glimpse of his potential prey. The sweet smell of pine brought back fond memories of his youth. He loved the sweet aromas of the forest. The distinctive scents of the wild animals, the collection of flowers and sages, and the gratifying smell of the end-of-day fire with the day's hunt roasting on the spit provided a tapestry of pleasure that Leo had come to enjoy in his years of training. It was that training, that Leo hoped had finally prepared him to defeat the Nephi.

Three shots—maybe four—sent toward the heart of the Nephi would bring him down, but Leo would then have to escape the rage of the lion horses. His escape wasn't certain, but he was confident in his stealth in the forest. He would trust what his master had taught him to bring him safely home at sunrise the next day.

Leo tested his position and steadied his stance. He placed his right hand against the hollow between the trees and pushed himself back quietly. With his feet shoulder-length apart, his right foot pointed directly toward the Nephi, who was seated on the stump, as Leo had hoped. Leo had been to this place and spied out this evening ritual before.

The lion horses paced, bowed, and pranced about the Nephi tirelessly for hours. The fire burned bright and long while this ceremony went on. The somber-faced 'Sons-of-darkness' were all dressed in black, as they meekly, and quickly worked to keep the fire going. They kept their heads down and never looked at the Nephi or the lion horses.

Two women wearing long red robes continuously beat the fire with long-handled brooms. They reminded Leo of witches. He half expected them to slip their brooms between their legs and fly off into the night. They wore gold-trimmed sashes about their necks. Chicken bones hung from the fringe on the sashes. Leo couldn't see all this from where he was, but he had been closer several times before. He used those times to test his skills of stealth and get a better look at the pattern of the nightly rituals. Leo knew that once they had gone to the nightly pattern, it would not be long until they chose to strike the village just a mile away. He must not fail. Too much was at risk for the village downstream.

To take out the Nephi before he attacked the village, is why he had trained so zealously. His zeal and skill is why he was chosen, and why he was there that night to stop what the Nephi and his lion horses had intended to do, once they set upon that village. Leo returned his attention to his position behind the twin trees. He took deep, slow breathes. He set his eyes upon the proud Nephi.

He removed his long bow from his back, and with his right hand, brought it up to his sight line. He steadied his gaze and envisioned the first arrow leaving its seat and flying to its mark. Leo placed his first arrow in its nocking point. With ease, he drew back on the mighty bow. He rested his left thumb and little finger against his cheek. The other three fingers held the bow string steady.

Leo's eyes darted back and forth across the plane of his vision. Nothing was out of place. Seconds from now, his mission would be complete. The Watchers had assured Leo that the Apollyon, the destroyer, would be held back this time. Once more his eyes scanned the field.

Thwish! Leo loosed the arrow, and his cat-like reflexes were set in motion. His rapid symphony of movement was stunning. As soon as the first arrow was loosed toward its mark, his hand moved back toward the quiver. Almost quicker than a blink, three arrows flew silently toward the Nephi. Leo had the fourth pulled and ready as the first arrow sunk with precision deep into the barrel chest of the large Nephi. Leo's eyesight was keen, and he could see the fiery pupils of the Nephi's eyes grow wide as it tried to determine the cause of the sudden intense pain in its chest. Before the Nephi even had time to move, the second arrow was following the first into the same place in its chest.

The Nephi's huge hand grabbed hard at the hole in its chest. The strength of the bow sent the first two arrows clean through its body. The third arrow struck the hand that was over the painful hole in its chest. The calloused hand slowed the speed of the third arrow, but now the Nephi's hand was pierced through and held tight to its bleeding chest.

The Nephi howled and roared in pain. Anger raged from within him. The ungodly roar of a mighty, enraged lion pierced the evening silence of the forest. The fourth arrow struck home, too. The Nephi had started to rise, so the fourth arrow was lodged in its hip. It struck hard at his pelvic bone and shattered it to pieces inside the joint.

The Nephi raged again. The lion horses roared with him as they stared on in shame. Their leader had been struck as they danced around him.

Leo's aim was true. Two arrows pierced the heart of the Nephi. He would die that night.

The hip shot was more good fortune for Leo. The Nephi couldn't run, and its left hand was severely wounded as well. If Leo dared fire another shot, the lion horses would be able to determine his position.

Leo watched them howl some more. They could see the mortal danger their leader was in and pranced in desperation, wondering what to do. They wanted to defend the Nephi but could see he was mortally wounded and dared not leave him.

Leo saw the 'Sons-of-darkness' over to the side cower in fright at what was happening. The rage of the lion horses would soon turn on the cowering men. There was nothing Leo could do for them. He had hit his mark. The wounds were mortal, and the lion horses would wait to see their master die. After that, they would kill the men and pursue whoever took the life of their master. Leo knew he probably had about ten minutes to get safely away. It would be enough time. He would be resting on the soft down mattress of his cabin bed in the morning, dreaming sweet dreams of his arrows finding their mark.

Leo glanced back once more to be sure he wasn't being followed yet. A small smile turned up the edges of his mouth. He turned, and his leather moccasins padded swiftly toward his home several miles away.

As Leo stepped off the sidewalk with Amanda by his side, he remembered his dreams of the past week. They had been the same every night. He was sure it was him in the dream, but he was much older. He didn't recognize the woods, nor did he understand how he could have learned such skill in hunting, and archery. He wished he was such a brave and skillful warrior, but he knew he wasn't.

CHAPTER TWENTY-FOUR

The Watcher Comes

Leo and Amanda walked together in the back of the group of friends on their way to the bonfire in the middle of the dirt field. The sun had set almost an hour earlier. Moths fluttered about in the night, chasing after streetlights and flashlights. A few of the kids brought flashlights after being pestered by their parents to do so. Those with flashlights became favorites of everyone around them. The tree roots, boulders, dips, and ruts along the way made for uneasy going. Many of the kids weren't used to walking in the dark. They muttered and complained as they stubbed their toes or tripped in unseen divots along the way.

The size of the throng made Leo feel secure. Trailing behind such a noisy troop of kids made him sure that whoever was out at the fire wouldn't be surprised this time.

"Everyone sure is making a lot of noise, huh, Leo?" Amanda pointed out.

"Yeah, no surprising anyone at their fire this time." Leo smiled at her.

"Do you think it's them out there?" Amanda asked.

"You mean the teenagers who took Blaine?"

"Yeah—or what about the big kid, the one you call the Nephi?"

"I don't know, but I kind of hope so."

Amanda turned and gave Leo a surprised look. “Why?”

“Well, with all these people around, I don’t think anything bad will happen. I was nervous to come out here at first, but now I realize this is great, with everybody walking out with us.”

“If it is them . . .” Amanda paused.

Leo waited and then prodded her to go on. “What?”

“Why so open this time? They’re not being secretive. It’s like we are being invited. That girl even waved at us to come out.”

“Maybe it’s a trap!” Leo snickered. Amanda smacked him when he did.

“Oh, never mind; go ahead and laugh. From what little I have seen, these kids are up to no good.” Amanda looked ahead and could see that some of the kids were getting close to the edge of the fire. “We’re almost there, Leo.”

Leo looked up. As he did, he saw his brother and Louis running back to find him.

“Right here, Blaine,” Leo called out to his brother.

“Leo, we should stick close. We don’t know who this group is or what they’re up to. It’s best if we stick together.”

“Come up with us to the front,” Blaine instructed.

“Really?” Leo protested mildly. *I do not want to go to the front. I’m the one they are looking for.* He wanted to scream it to his brother but kept the thought to himself.

“Yes, it’s where Eric and Frank and the other guys are. You too, Amanda; you should come with us.” Blaine waved for Amanda to hurry and come with them. She and Leo jogged to the front of the pack of kids. It was the biggest nighttime hike the friends had ever had. They would have stopped and ran back, if they knew what was to come next.

Frank and Eric were at the front of the pack. They stopped in front of two burly-looking teens dressed in black. The broad-shouldered teens stood firm with surly faces and muscled arms folded across their chests. They stood guard between Leo and his friends and the raging fire just thirty feet behind them. Leo and the others didn't pose any threat to anyone at the fire, but the burly duo held their position firm. Leo and Amanda scurried up behind Blaine, who had settled in next to Frank. Blaine whispered something to Frank and then looked back at Leo.

"Leo, I thought you weren't coming for a second," Frank stated.

"Is Leo here?" It was more of a bellow than a question that came from one of the muscled teens standing guard.

Leo cringed at the thought of the burly guards knowing his name. The normally brash Frank was a little intimidated by the two large kids who stood in front of him.

"Leo; yeah, Leo's here," Frank answered, trying to look sure of himself.

Immediately, a sudden wind gust whistled from behind Leo and the kids. It tugged, pulled, and whipped at their hair and clothing as it tore past, dragging leaves and dirt with it. As quick as it came, the sudden gust was gone.

What was that? Leo wondered. All the kids looked around, wondering the same thing. At that moment, a great crash was heard at the fire. Someone had tossed a huge log onto the already huge fire.

Leo looked toward the disturbance at the fire. He was chilled to see four red-robed women beating at the edges of the fire with long-handled brooms. They seemed to move in a symphony of ritual. One at a time, they took their brooms, dipped them into the ocean of raging flames, and raised the brooms high over their heads to send a shower of sparks into the night sky. All four were synchronized in their motions, intent on stirring a flurry of sparks and embers ascending into the night. A couple dozen black-clothed teenagers were seated crossed-legged in a circle around the fire.

"Leo, come sit with me," a voice boomed out from somewhere around the fire. "I'm here, Leo. Come sit with me." The voice rumbled like thunder.

Leo saw where the voice came from. On the other side of the fire, the tall teenager sat on a wooden stump. Two other teens in long black robes flanked the Nephi on either side. The now-familiar lettering was written on each sleeve of the dark robes. Leo was sure he was the young Nephi the Shah had spoken of. Leo still had not determined what he thought the Nephi was, but he believed it was possible that he wasn't as human as he looked. It was hard to fathom, but Leo thought he might be some kind of animal and human cross breed.

"Leo." Amanda stood close at his side, grabbed his arm tightly, and pleaded. "Stay with me."

Blaine was part of a tight circle of friends who all faced Leo. "Let's think about this, bro." Blaine and the others looked concerned. The broad-shouldered guards, the freaky blast of wind, and the thundering voice from the Nephi took the courage from everyone.

"All of you—Leo, bring all of your friends to me," the Nephi commanded again.

Without hesitation, Leo, Blaine, and the others obeyed. The thickset guards directed all the kids to a place in front of the Nephi. With Leo, Blaine, and Amanda in front, all of the kids sheepishly took up a spot on the ground between the raging fire and the Nephi. The four women who had been fanning the flames stopped and watched the procession of young kids go by. As the kids passed one of the red-robed women, Amanda squeezed Leo's arm.

Leo glanced over. Amanda nodded her head toward one of the women leaning on her broom. It was Alice, the librarian's assistant who Amanda had insisted that Leo should not trust. Leo looked at Alice, who returned his stare with a cold, icy glare. *A witch; Alice is one of the witches from my dream,* Leo thought. He tore his eyes away from Alice's icy glare and looked back at Amanda. She was terror-struck. "It will be fine, Amanda." Leo said. "I hope."

Seeing Alice made Leo realize there must be a tangled web of devious intent among the groups of teens. Were they plotting together to help the Nephi?

Stupid and foolish, the Shah said. Why did we come out to this trap? Leo screamed in silent fury at himself.

"At last, Leo, welcome." The Nephi spoke in his unnaturally loud and thunderous voice. This was no ordinary teenager; his voice alone made Leo realize there was something deep and sinister about him.

Blaine hadn't said anything about his voice. Is it different now? Leo stared back without answering. After a few seconds of uneasy silence, he tore his eyes away from the Nephi and surveyed his surroundings. *How do we get out of here?* Leo felt responsible for getting Amanda, Blaine, and his friends away from the fire. Then Leo remembered something. *There is no fire in his eyes.*

"Scimitars!" the Nephi shouted. The two black-robed teens returned to the Nephi's side.

Leo recognized the word. The teens each held a broad-bladed sword, called a scimitar, across their chests. Several gasps and moans came from Leo's friends. A few started to whimper and cry, while another could be heard quietly calling out for his mom. A chilling anxiety stirred them all.

The frightening-looking blades glistened and reflected the fire off their polished steel. A couple of boys could be heard sobbing. Leo started to look back to see who it was, but his eyes didn't get past Amanda.

Her faced was dipped toward the ground, her eyes were closed, but her cheeks were streaked with tears. Her lips moved as she muttered something under breath. Her whole body shook with fear. "Pray, Amanda!" Leo said, but knew she already was.

Leo knew he had to try something. He stood and spoke out. "I'm Leo, sir. What do you . . . want with me . . . and my friends?" The normally timid Leo tried to mask the tremor in his voice.

"I want nothing to do with your friends, and as for you, I know who you are!" Anger stirred in the thunderous response of the Nephi. Leo's boldness angered him. His voice boomed louder than before.

Leo didn't take his eyes off the Nephi. He caught a glimmer of something he remembered from his dream. The pupils of the Nephi's eyes began to flicker with tiny flames.

In a calmer voice, the Nephi spoke again. "Leo, I can have your friends removed." He looked to his right and stared at the scimitar held by the black-robed guard. "I only have an interest in you, Leo."

"What are you?" The question jumped out of Leo's mouth before he could think to hold his tongue.

"This is why you have been chosen, Leo. You see things that others do not."

"What's in the book I saw you holding in my dreams?"

The tiny flickers in the Nephi's eyes surged brighter. With a questioning look, he asked Leo, "So, you are a seer, then?" He looked at Leo—the timid little boy—and marveled.

"I don't know anything about seeing and stuff; I just think I should take my brother and my friends back home now. I don't want to know anything about what you are doing here. We're sorry for coming out here." Leo spoke boldly to the Nephi, who was more than the teen he appeared to be.

"Do you really want to know what I am, Leo?" the Nephi asked.

"Um . . . no, sir. Not really, I think. We're just kids; we were playing. May we just go now?"

"No! You are chosen, Leo. You are a seer. Your friends will be removed." The Nephi turned to the teen on his right, who stood statue-like. "Remove them all!" he shouted. At his command, the sword-wielding guards stepped toward Leo and his friends. Leo, who had stood as he spoke to the Nephi, stumbled backward and fell onto the ground.

The black-clad teens rose to encircle the younger kids while the robed women restarted their fire ritual. As their brooms struck the flames, their motions sent more sparks into the sky. Panic struck Leo's friends. They dared to look longingly around for any sign of hope or escape.

Another freaky rush of wind returned to tear at their clothes and hair. As the gust tore over the fire, it sent a shower of embers upon the teens. The kids responded with screams at the embers and the sound of the intense wind. The kids had never felt a hurricane before, but they thought it couldn't be stronger or more terrifying than this.

Leo lifted his head with both hands, shielding his eyes. *Where did this raging wind come from?*

The black-clad teens and the women lay flat on their faces, hiding themselves from the fury of the wind. The sword-wielding teens dropped their swords and rolled on the ground, patting feverishly at the flames that started to engulf their black robes.

Leo saw the Nephi. His eyes had become flames, as Leo had seen in his dreams. The Nephi shook his right fist in anger at the sky. Behind the Nephi's head, Leo saw a thick mass of clouds rolling in and swallowing up the stars in the sky. The raging wind from behind and the roiling black mass of clouds were about to collide right where they all sat.

Lighting streaked and pierced the mass of clouds. The star-filled sky was soon covered by the mass of clouds, a spectacular display of lightning, and claps of thunder. The thunder immediately pounded everyone's eardrums. The kids were caught in the most frightening lightning storm they had ever seen. Bolts struck and singed the ground and sent up spires of smoke from the places it struck. The ground shook and trembled all around them.

Leo looked over at his brother on his left. Blaine and the others lay face down, shrinking from the storm. A blinding streak from the sky struck the giant oak over Leo's head. The flash blinded his eyes with light, he couldn't see anything. The thunder and heat that followed were fiercely intense.

Leo knew the giant oak had taken a direct hit. He heard the splitting and sickening crack of the tree right over his head. He heard it breaking loose, but he was frozen, too horror-struck to move. Leo cringed under the shield of his arms and hoped to be spared. He peeked through the slender defense of his arms and saw the Nephi now shaking both his fists toward the storm.

Leo saw the huge branch come crashing down on top of the Nephi. He heard the lion's mighty roar as the branch pierced the Nephi's body and pinned him to the ground. The jagged and splintered spear from the oak tore away and went hurling into the heart of the Nephi. His lungs expelled a final breath.

Almost gone, the Nephi weakly turned his head to look over at Leo. The flames and rage of his eyes were replaced by the pain and certainty of death. He clenched his weakened fist at Leo, meekly pounded it on the ground once, and closed his eyes. His head fell with a thud to the ground.

Another mighty crack of thunder rattled the sky. Leo looked up at the roiling dark clouds. In the mass of darkness, he saw a giant creature of light standing firmly in the sky in front of the dark cauldron of clouds above his head. The creature was brilliant beyond any wonder Leo had ever imagined. It had six magnificent wings. Two wings covered its feet, two were folded over its chest, and the other two waved slowly in the evening sky. Leo felt the gentle push of wind upon his face when the wings were brought down toward the earth.

The mighty creature held a book in his right hand. With slight shifts in the stroke of his wings, the angelic vision drifted down to stand on the ground in front of Leo.

Leo was stunned and silent, but he didn't feel fear. *Who are you? What are you? Are you one of the Watchers the Shah said would protect me?* Leo gazed in wonder at the enormous Watcher. *Is that what you are . . . are you a Watcher?*

A crack of thunder sounded from the lips of the vision. Leo crumpled to the ground at the words he spoke. "Only a few choose to see; far fewer are chosen to be seers. You shall be trained to see, Leo. What you have seen is a foretelling of the war that comes to the earth. The combatants are mighty beyond your dreams Leo, but the sons of man will play an important part in the war. The Destroyer leads his forces against the sons of man, and will use the Nephilim to deceive many. In your dreams, you shall receive understanding of what is in your future Leo."

The six-winged glorious vision stretched out his right hand, which held a book toward Leo. The eagle-like claws on the hand of the Watcher delicately but firmly held the book. Not a claw pierced any of the cover that looked to be made of soft, tanned leather.

Leo's fear at the thunderous words eased, and he stretched his hand out to grab the book. As he touched the book, a brilliant rainbow of color and light flashed before him. He recoiled from the blast of light. He rubbed his eyes and felt for the book, but it was gone.

Leo's eyes recovered from the flash, but the angelic vision was gone. The most beautiful, and fearsome creature he could ever imagine was gone. The book he tried to grasp was gone too, along with the six-winged vision of glory. He looked up in the sky. The lightning and thunder cleared, and the thick blackness broke, allowing patches of stars to show through.

Leo looked in front of him at the massive fallen branch. He was surprised to see that the Nephi was gone, too. Leo eased himself up on his feet, stepped around his brother, and carefully walked over to the broken branches that were in front of him. He cautiously looked under and around the leaves and branches to be sure. The Nephi was gone. The thunder, lightning, and brilliant creature were gone.

It began to rain hard. Leo heard Amanda shriek. Blaine and his friends hastily picked themselves up off the ground as little rivulets and streams began to flow across the ground around them.

CHAPTER TWENTY-FIVE

Chosen to See

Amanda had a huge smile on her face when Leo looked over at her. The terror was gone from her face. "Oh no! Leo, we're getting soaked." Amanda giggled with excitement.

"Leo!" Blaine hollered.

"Yeah, Blaine?"

"Make sure we're all together. Let's get out of here, bro!"

"Quiet man!" Louis yelled. "I'll grab the rear; you guys lead everybody out. Me and Frank will make sure everyone finds their way through the mud." Louis was such a fun and smart-alecky type that it sounded odd to hear him take charge and look out for some of his buddies.

"Thanks, Louis. We'll get them started out," Leo answered.

Leo's buddies were all up on their feet, scrambling to find a good trail that would lead to the street. The fire that a few minutes ago had sent sparks and embers into the sky had been doused by the downpour. Massive plumes of steam and smoke now billowed up into the night.

The black-clad teens and the women, who had stirred the flames, were running off in a jumbled effort to find cover. *They all look lost now,* Leo thought. *Do they know the Nephi is dead? Do they know he is gone? Who will they follow now?* Leo almost felt sorry for them as they seemed to panic and looked helpless. *The Shah said they were fools; they sure look to be that now.*

Amanda ran to Leo, grabbed his hand, and pulled him along with the others who found their way through the mud and streams of rain water. "I'm soaked; are you?" Amanda giggled and laughed.

"Just a little." Leo laughed at her silly question. He enjoyed holding her hand and seeing her happy smile.

Amanda steadied herself in Leo's grip as they carefully chose their steps on the slippery soil. Leo looked back as they ran.

"They're coming, Leo. Frank and Louis will make sure they all get out of the rain," Amanda said.

"I know; I was just wondering about the teenagers."

"Oh, they were nice, huh?" Amanda asked.

Leo turned and looked at her with surprise. *What does she mean by that? She does seem pretty happy after the scare she just had. Did she miss what just happened?*

As they ran, Leo tried to think through what had just happened. *Where did the Nephi go? Was it just an accident that killed him or that huge winged Watcher? What was that book he handed to me, and where did it disappear to?*

Leo looked at Amanda and the huge smile on her face. "You're enjoying this, aren't you?" he asked.

"I'm freezing and completely soaked, but this is so much fun!" Her voice grew louder as she finished her sentence. "Leo, look out!" she yelled.

Leo looked down just in time to save his toes from slamming into a big rock. He slipped a little, but Amanda pulled at his arm and helped him as they both stumbled forward.

"Finally!" Amanda exclaimed as they pounded their muddy feet onto the pavement of the street. As they continued to run, they slammed their feet hard with each step to force some of the mud off their feet.

"Guys, let's go to my house," Blaine yelled back at those who had followed close behind. "Stomp your feet before you go in, though!"

The boys' mother was out again and wouldn't be expected back for hours. Blaine pulled out his key, inserted it into the lock, and turned. At the click of the tumblers, he flung the door open to let the flood of soaking kids pour in to find cover from the rain. "Stay off the couch, guys. Just sit on the floor. I'll go look for some towels so we can dry off."

Leo and Amanda spilled inside with the rest of them but headed into the kitchen to avoid the crush of kids in the living room. Amanda still clung tightly to Leo's hand. "That was fun, huh, Leo? That rain felt so good, huh?" Amanda had a sheepish grin on her face as she brought Leo's arm up to her forehead to dry her dripping head.

Leo smiled, looked back at her, and then let his eyes wander to all of the others he could see. *Did she see everything that I just saw? Has she forgotten? Is it the same with the others here?*

"What was so fun, Amanda?" Leo asked.

"Oh, the whole thing. The walk in the field and the rain—didn't you like that, Leo?" Amanda held his hand with both of hers and shivered. "I wish we had that fire still; now I'm cold."

Leo looked at her smiling face and smiled back. He looked over the counter to find his brother in the mass of shivering friends in the living room. Blaine passed out towels to everyone. They were all laughing and smiling as if they all had just had a great time. *Why is everyone acting like nothing more happened than getting caught in the rain? Don't they remember the huge swords?*

Leo looked back at Amanda. *Doesn't she remember how much she trembled in fear at the sight of those swords? What about the thunder and lightning—the cracking and breaking of that huge branch that pierced and crushed the Nephi, the witch women in their red robes, and the creature with six wings? Don't they remember all that? Did all of that go unnoticed by them?* Leo looked at the faces of all his friends in the living room and those who spilled into the kitchen with him and Amanda. *It couldn't all have escaped them—or was it somehow forgotten?*

Leo remembered that all the kids had been face-down, shaking in fear for what they thought was about to happen to them. Now they seemed to only be talking about the huge fire and the sudden rain that doused it and chased them all back to the house. *Was I dreaming again? What just happened?*

"Catch, bro!" Blaine yelled at Leo as he sent a towel flying toward him and Amanda. Amanda grabbed at it as it flew by and wrapped her and Leo in it. He blushed, though he was happy to be wrapped in a dry towel with her. He thought about what the winged Watcher had told him. *Few are chosen to see. You shall be trained to see.*

What was it that Amanda said about the boy Samuel? He heard the voice of God? 'In your dreams, you shall receive understanding of what is in your future Leo.' That's what the six-winged creature said.

Leo looked at Amanda and smiled. She smiled back at him.

"Those teenagers were nice, huh, Leo? It's too bad the rain came so quickly after they let us join them at the fire."

Leo just gave her a blank stare.

"What?" Amanda asked. "Didn't you think they turned out to be nice?" Leo shrugged.

She doesn't remember any of it. Leo guessed that Amanda, Blaine, and his buddies had not seen or somehow had forgotten most of what happened at the fire some thirty minutes ago.

Surely Blaine remembers something. I'm going to have to ask Amanda more about that kid, Samuel. I wonder if he was the only one who heard the voice. I'll ask her tomorrow.

Leo smiled as he watched his brother dancing around the table with a towel on his head, making fun of the Shah. The kids laughed and enjoyed Blaine's mimicking of the friendly old man at the liquor store.

Leo settled in and enjoyed the show Blaine put on for everyone. He enjoyed the warmth of the towel and Amanda's shoulder against his.

Leo dreamt he was standing in the field, where he remembered seeing the dance of the lion-horses around the Nephi, before his life was ended by the four arrows, sent by the archer. The archer had looked like Leo, all grown up, and trained to battle wicked creatures full of evil intent.

There was no sign of the lion-horses or the Nephi having been there, but he knew the place well, because he had been there so many times, in preparation for the kill, for which he had trained those many months.

Leo remembered the dreams of his training. He realized the dreams would become real. Someday he would begin to train for real, no longer just in dreams.

I am being trained to see, the Watcher said. Leo remembered. "Apparently I'm being trained to fight too." His spoken words broke the silence of the quiet meadow, in the middle of the thick forest.

A steady breeze blew at his hair and clothing. He turned to his right from where the breeze came and saw the stunning brilliance of the glorious six-winged Watcher from his dreams. The breeze gusted toward Leo as the mighty angel pushed his wings earthward, and it ebbed when it pulled its wings back to recoil for another push.

Leo's hair and clothing moved back and forth in unison with the push and pull of the giant wingspan of the Watcher. Leo was learning to recognize the wind gusts that were a sign of the Watcher's presence.

The angel glided to a stop, less than ten feet from where Leo stood in the open field. Leo's knees buckled and his legs lost all strength, before he collapsed face first as the magnificent creature drew close.

"I have been sent from the High and Lofty One, who inhabits eternity, to bring you another message. Young warrior, your training as a seer has begun. The battle is not yours to fight and it never will be, but you have been called to be a seer for the Most High. The outcome is in the hands of the One who rules the heavens. You have been called out for his purpose. You have been chosen to be in a battle with the powers and principalities of the returning dark rebellion. These foes are too powerful for you, but you will be made ready. In your weakness you will be made strong by 'El Elyon' the Most High God, the One who inhabits Eternity."

"I have defeated the Nephilim who sought your life, but there will be more. Many Nephilim are now being prepared for the dark plan that is soon to come upon the sons of man. El Elyon will give you understanding in these things."

"El Elyon? Is he a god?" Leo wondered. His answer came immediately as the Watcher read his thoughts.

"He is God Most High and there is no god beside Him. He is the Creator and possessor of Heaven and Earth."

"It is he who has called you to be a dream warrior that you might warn those who sleep. Already your home has been marked by the sons of darkness and they will seek to stop you, but you are watched and protected by the servants of the Most High."

"The symbol on my front door;" Leo thought.

"As in the days of the sons of Eli, when young Samuel was being trained to see, the leaders again, have corrupted themselves and have grown fat on their lies and deceit. Their children, the sons of darkness lead astray the foolish. They follow the fallen sons of God in the dark rebellion. It is time for the sons of man to awaken out of their slumber and be made ready for the battle.

You have been chosen to see while there is yet light."

"The time of darkness is coming, which the ancient texts have prophesied. It will not be stopped; it is for the cleansing of the righteous and so that the rebellious will be without excuse. 'El Elyon' the Most High God, has shown you what is soon to come upon those who slumber and sleep. The destroyer is mounting up the Nephilim again as the days of his judgment draw close."

"It was the voice of God that young Samuel heard as he slept, and it is again the voice of God that you, young Leo, have heard. Young Samuel's days were growing dark, but your days, young Leo, will be darker still. He who has ears to hear, let him hear, for the voice of the Most High God is about to bring thunder upon the deaf. You have been given one book Leo, the Word of 'El Elyon'. Take it and do not lose grasp of it."

The vision of the Watcher faded and Leo was again in his kitchen, wrapped in a towel with Amanda.

He looked out toward the living room and saw his brother Blaine. He was still dancing around the living room with the towel on his head. Leo looked to his left and Amanda's smiling face was inches away.

"Who will I try to wake up first?" Leo thought.